F(

Copyrigh

ISBN:

Imprint: I...

All Rights Reserved

Printed in the USA

Cover design by Grim Poppy

WARNING

This is extreme splatterpunk horror.
If you do not like extreme splatterpunk horror... you will not like this book. It is only intended for mature readers.

For the Sake Of

FOR

THE

SAKE

OF

An extreme horror novella by
Judith Sonnet

For the Sake Of

For the Sake Of

To

Christy Aldridge

The best ghoul around

For the Sake Of

Part One
Plumbing

Chapter One
Play Stupid Games

Greta Hilligloss answered the phone the second it chirped. She had been staring at it since its arrival in an unmarked paper bag on her back doorstep. Along with the phone, there had been a picture that had filled her with dread.

Her husband, Donnie, had been missing for two days. Greta's parents made no allusions toward their suspicions.

"He's run off, hasn't he? That's what he did, the dog. Run off. Found his-self some tart to gallivant about with, eh?"

They didn't care that it made her eyes well up with tears. They pressed the issue like a button.

"He's been cheating, hasn't he? You can tell us. No need leaving him unsullied if he done up and run off on you, huh?"

Greta didn't care what they said.

Donnie wasn't cheating on her.

Not anymore.

Yes, there had been that time with Eloise at work. But Eloise was a one-off. Donnie had sworn to remain true to Greta, even if she wasn't as exciting or as plump as Eloise.

She was almost relieved to discover—via the Polaroid stowed in with the phone—that her Donnie had been kidnapped. Until, of course, the horror of the situation dawned on her.

Donnie was pictured in his briefs. His jiggly tummy—which she loved to put her head against—was scuffed with blue bruises. His right eye was sealed shut and was gummy with blood. His nose was broken, and his mouth hung open, exposing shattered teeth. He had been beaten. Maybe he had put up more of a fight than his abductors expected. Or maybe—and this thought was monumentally worse—they had beaten him for fun.

He was strapped to the chair with bungee cables and duct tape. A gun was pointed to his head. The assailant couldn't be seen. But his skin was white, and his nails were long, like a goblin's. She realized that was exactly what she was picturing. A fairytale troll, holding her Donnie hostage.

Greta turned the Polaroid over and found a message written in black ink:

We'll Call You. No Police.

Greta sat at her dinner table and waited for the phone to ring. All the while, she knotted her hands together and considered waking her parents. They were snoozing in the guestroom, having taken a nap after tea. She figured they would be up in a mere thirty minutes.

If they saw the picture they'd be sure to call the police, no matter how hard Greta pleaded. And then where would they be? Would they discover Donnie dead in a ditch, the gun having been discharged by the yellow-clawed hooligan?

Greta sighed and looked at herself in the mirror. She looked haggard and sickly. Her eyes had turned sour, and her cheeks were pale. Her blue lips trembled around her un-brushed teeth. Her red hair was stringy, like a sock-doll's.

She couldn't help but wonder what Eloise was up to today—

—the phone rang.

In a hushed but urgent whisper, Greta answered: "Hullo?"

"Hello." The voice was American. Male.

"Hullo?" Greta asked, impatiently.

"Hello? Can you hear me?"

"Yes. I can hear you." Greta ground her teeth together.

"Good. But I can't hear you very well. Can I test something out here?" He was so polite, she felt as if she was on a call with a solicitor.

"Y-yes."

"Can you say something for me?"

"Yes."

"Can you say: 'I eat shit'?"

Greta frowned. She never swore. Even when Donnie asked her to speak dirty to him, all she could muster was a weak "I like your... *pee-niss.*"

"No, no, no... wait! Say: 'I eat shit and I like it'?"

"I'll do no such thing!" Greta blurted.

"Ah, ah. Ah." The American voice rasped. "You might want to start doing what I say, Greta. Because... Donnie's life may depend on it."

"What have you done with him?" Greta asked.

"Nothing, yet. He's a real hog, isn't he? We had a helluva time roping him up. But we aren't interested in hurting him anymore. Are we?"

We? How many people were involved in this? She hadn't even thought that a secondary person had had to take the picture while the goblin pointed the gun at her husband's oval head.

"So, Greta, this is how it'll go. I'll tell you to do something, and you do it. If you complete three tasks, I'll award Donnie his freedom. If you fail the first task, we cut off a limb of your choosing. If you fail the second task... we castrate him. If you fail the third task... we kill him. If you alert the police or your pop an' ma... we kill him. If you understand the rules of the game then say: 'I eat shit and I like it'."

Greta was stunned. Not only by the perverse commands but by the cavalier tone with which the young man spoke. It was as if he was playing solitaire. As if this was a meddlesome way to pass the time. It made it all feel so unreal. So freakish.

And yet, when Greta closed her eyes she imagined Donnie on the other end of the line. Tied to the chair and biting into his tongue with fear. His eyes bloodshot with panic. Maybe he was even soiling himself, oh god! Greta wished she could pull him out of these dire straits by force of will alone.

But if she didn't do this, he'd be dead. They'd kill him and who knew whether or not his corpse would ever be found. Greta had no choice but to play along.

"Okay." She said.

"Hmm?"

"I said... 'Okay'."

"That isn't what I asked you to say."

Greta scowled. She had been raised not to swear. Good girls didn't befoul their mouth with crass words. She may as well have converted her mouth into a truck stop bathroom as soon as say a dirty word. But she had to, for Donnie's sake.

"I eat shit... and I like it."

"Good." The voice on the other end seethed obscenely. "Let's do a practice round, okay? Just to get into the spirit of things. There's no risk for Donnie here. He'll be fine whether you pass or fail. Well... minus a few fingers."

Greta nodded.

"I want you to take your Bible and rip out a page. Just a single page. And I want you to wipe

11

your ass with it."

Greta walked upstairs with all the dread of a prisoner on death row. If swearing was a terrible sin, then this was an unforgivable one. She could only hope that her God would be able to understand, given the circumstances.

"You're going to take a video. The phone can do that. Everything will need to be confirmed via picture and video. You got that?"

"Y-yes."

"Good."

"Who are you?" Greta asked as she took the doorknob and pressed into her and her husband's bedroom. Hanging above their bed sat a crucifix. Christ frowned down at her, dismayed by what she was about to do.

"You can call me 'Daddy'." The voice on the other end of the phone broke into hysterics.

Greta sighed and wiped a tear away with the back of her hand. Her knuckles dug into her eyes and drew up more fluid. She hadn't realized it, but she was sobbing. *That's because this is a violation. He's assaulting you from a distance.* She felt her stomach rumble as she opened her nightstand and pulled out her favorite Bible. A baby-blue cover with her name inscribed in cursive. She opened it and leafed through the pages. After what was about to happen, she didn't know if she'd ever find solace within the word of God ever again.

"I'm waiting." Daddy said without emotion.

Greta lifted her skirt and pulled down her bottoms. She set the phone up and searched for the camera app. After finding it, she was disgusted to look at her own face. It was smeared in runny mucus.

Goddamn you, whoever you are. You sick, disgusting pig.

Greta hit record.

She held the Bible up, displaying the page she had chosen. It was from the book of Numbers. A book she had never really understood in the first place. She grabbed the page and sensitively tore it out. There was a visceral reaction. Her lips drew back and her eyes pinched shut. It was as if she expected God to smite her in that very second. After the page was torn loose, she buried it beneath her skirts and wiped. Just as she was commanded. She was careful not to show any skin on camera. Afterwards, she held it up so it could be seen. Much to her shame, there was a little brown streak on one of the corners.

She tossed the paper, sent the video, and buried her face in her hands. Her shoulders shuddered as she wept.

After composing herself, she picked up the phone and placed it against her head:

"Well?"

"Very good, Greta! You're really catching onto the spirit of the game! Donnie's awful proud of you, and I think a bit more confident too. Wouldn't you say, Don?"

A muffled groan rose up from the other end of the line.

Greta put her hand against her mouth and breathed in deeply. Her terror was so intense; it could have snapped her heart.

"We're playing for real from here on out." Daddy said. "And remember, Donnie's limbs depend on it."

Greta nodded.

"I want you to go downstairs now, and pick out the sharpest knife you have,"

Greta walked downstairs in a daze. She didn't even know if this was real anymore. It felt like a terrible nightmare. The sort of dream she'd wake up all sweaty from. Greta used to have night terrors as a child. They'd make her scream so loud it woke her parents.

But this was worse.

This was... *inescapable*.

"What do you want me to do with it?" She asked.

"Do you have it yet?"

"No." She chirped.

"Then don't ask questions."

Greta wandered into the kitchen on slow feet. She pulled a drawer open and rifled through it. Greta wasn't much of a cook and Donnie was even less of one. They survived on a diet of take-out and microwaved meals. It was where Donnie had gotten his lovely belly from. So, knives were scarce. The sharpest thing she had was a black-handled steak knife she used to cut the plastic on cardboard packages with. She picked it up with shaky fingers. "I've got it." She shuddered.

"Good." Daddy took a deep breath, as if he was considering what he wanted her to do next. "I want you... to cut off your ear. Like Van Gogh."

"What?" Greta shrieked.

"Prove to Donnie you love him. Cut off your ear. And then, send a picture..."

"I don't want to... I don't want to do *that*!"

"It's either you cut off an ear, or we cut something off of Donnie. Which do you like more, his left or his right arm?"

"No! No! No. No. No. No. No. No. No. No."

"If you forfeit this task, we cut off a limb. Then we move onto the next one. It doesn't just stop, Greta. It never has and it never will. You gotta do it."

"No. No. No. No." Greta was hyperventilating.

Greta set the phone down.

"No. No. No."

She lifted the knife up and pulled her ear out by the lobe.

"No. No. No."

She put the knife beneath it.

"No. No. No."

"Greta?" The voice of her father came out from

15

behind her.

Greta ratcheted the knife up. It skimmed through the skin but bit sharply into the resistant cartilage. Hot blood slipped out from beside the blade and dribbled over Greta's shaking shoulder.

"NO!" Greta screamed and pulled the knife up, tearing with her hand as she went. The ear wasn't coming away easily. It wasn't like in the movies. Not at all.

She slapped the meaty leftovers of her right ear onto the kitchen table and screamed. It looked like she had pulled the dried pulp out from the bottom of an abandoned tub of orange juice. Just strings of flesh packed together above a puddle of blood.

"Greta, god, girl! What are you doing?" Her father roared. His hair was sticking out in odd angles and his eyes were crusty with sleep. He had been drawn out of bed by his daughter's wails.

Greta didn't respond. She picked up the cell-phone, snapped a picture of the dismembered ear, and then put the phone up to her remaining one.

"What next?" She asked, her voice a garbled mess. "What next you *TWISTED* FUCK?!"

Chapter Two
Tabby

Tabby had lost fifty pounds. Usually, she would have been proud of such a dramatic drop. But looking at herself in the mirror, she was like a living skeleton. It was the stress. It had made her eat like crazy, but she couldn't keep any of the weight. She threw up like a ballerina and tore her hair out like a mad scientist. There was no kidding herself. If there was anyone who looked like their child had been missing for the last eight and a half months, it was Tabby.

Tabitha Gilman Moss had been born –and she thought she would die—in Missouri. She looked the part, with her pasty white skin and dusty blonde hair pulled so far back it made her brow look all too smooth. She carried a drawl, rarely smiled, and smelled of goat-fur and dried dirt. She was a farmer, working the land she had inherited from her parents alongside her husband.

Thinking of Randy made her feel hollow inside.

He was gone. Not permanently, he had assured her, but isn't that how divorces started? She had read that a missing child would either tear a couple apart or pull them together. She wanted to talk to the lucky fucks that had managed to keep it together.

Maybe she'd throttle them.

Maybe she'd kiss their asses.

Either way, it would be a memorable meeting.

Tabby sighed and stepped out onto her front porch. She carried a mug of coffee and the morning paper, which had been waiting for her at the end of her gravel drive. She always retrieved it before she made her coffee.

Tabby sat down on her grandfather's rocking chair and opened the paper, hoping that somehow they had gotten an inside scoop before the police had notified her:

Riley Talbot Moss FOUND! Six-year-old girl discovered wandering through woods, lost and unharmed!

It was a fantasy that did more harm than good, but Tabby couldn't start her morning without a little hope. She sighed as she flipped through the pages. It was mostly fearmongering spliced with charming local tidbits. Garth Anders had hosted his annual pig-race and the winner was named Dottie. A new quilt barn was opening on main-street. And it looked like Shelly Darling was hosting another futile anti-mask rally. Tabby didn't really care about any of it. None of it pertained to Riley.

She remembered when her daughter had been front page news. Now, she wasn't even regulated to a sidebar. Eight months, and everyone assumed the worst. Tabby did too, but she couldn't allow herself to linger over it.

If Riley's dead, I'll commit suicide. She had thought in the early days of the search. Tabby now wondered if that ultimatum came with a caveat. Would Tabby commit suicide if Riley was *presumed* dead? Or did she have to *see* her daughter's six-year-old corpse before she blew her brains out?

She wondered what Randy was up to. He had gone upstate to spend a few weeks at his parents. Tabby did wish he was around. At the very least, he'd give her someone to be mad at other than herself. At the very best, maybe they'd reconcile and transform into one of those irritating couples that had pulled together after their child's disappearance. She doubted that, but still, it was a nice dream. Like the one she had where she opened the newspaper, and it told her exactly what she wanted to hear.

Her phone rang in her pocket. She pulled it out and looked at the screen, disappointed it wasn't Detective Brubaker with news on Riley's whereabouts. Instead, it was Randy. His ears must have been burning.

"Hello?" Tabby asked gruffly into the phone.

"Hey, Tabs. Are you doing okay today?" Randy

asked. She could hear bacon sizzling on the other end of the line. She had thought the coffee would cover her but now her mouth was feeling wet.

"I'm fine." Tabby growled and looked at her fingers. Her nails were getting unruly. She hadn't trimmed them in a few days. "What's up?"

"Just had a feeling." Randy was always having feelings. He was always worried that something was happening to Tabby... and yet, he hadn't had any preternatural urges the day Riley had disappeared from their front yard. What had he been working on that day? The plumbing in the basement toilet?

"Nope. I'm fine." Tabby sighed and rolled her tongue from one cheek to the other. "You want to tell me what's really going on?"

Randy sighed. His tone matched the sizzling bacon. Tabby could always read through his charades. It was no use pretending. "I just felt bad and thought I should check in. I didn't want you thinking I... you know... abandoned you."

"Well." Tabby bit her lower lip and glanced out at the farm. One of her goats was braying for attention. "Well, you kind of... did."

Randy breathed out deeply.

Randy Paul Moss was not the type of man Tabitha had expected to fall in love with. She had grown up around hicks and linebackers, and

Randy had been bullied by both. He was a smart guy that wore spectacles, carried a belly, and wore a thick beard. He was good with his hands, but better with his brains. He worked as a risk analyst for an insurance company. When he talked about work, it boggled Tabby's mind that he could even get through a single day of it without blowing up like that dude from *Scanners*. But, if opposites did attract, then that rule was definitely proven by Tabby and Randy. Until Riley had disappeared, their relationship had been rocksteady.

Tabby closed her eyes and tried to find an untainted memory. One where the three of them were together. She saw Riley sitting between them on a picnic blanket, her eyes glued to a picture book and her lips sculpted into a snaggletooth-ed smile. Tabby recalled the little dress she was wearing. Red with polka dots.

What had she been wearing the day she was abducted from their front yard? Randy had dressed her that morning. Tabby tried to remember what the police had said before they searched the woods:

"We're looking for a six-year-old girl with short, brown hair. She's wearing jeans and a blue Pony t-shirt! She answers to 'Riley', and she has a birthmark on the right side of her throat!" It had been announced into a bullhorn toward an audience of familiar faces. Folks from Tabby and

Randy's church had shown up to comb the woods. Most everyone from town was there too. There were a lot of strangers, but they were locals. They were all people Tabby would see at the supermarket for years afterwards. And she was sure that every time they saw her, they'd be thinking:

"There's that poor woman. I wonder if they ever found her kid."

"Tabby? Tabby? Are you there?" Randy was buzzing in her ear. Tabby shook her head and returned to the present. It was easy for her to get lost in her thoughts nowadays.

"Yes. Sorry. What?"

"I was just telling you I'm going to be another week up here." Randy said. "I was asking if that was okay with you."

"Yeah." Tabby pursed her lips and took a sip of her cooling coffee. "Yeah, I'll manage."

"Are you sure? I hate to think of you being on your own there—"

"No. It's okay. Take your time." Tabby set her coffee down and rocked back in her seat. She really wished this call would end. She had had enough of Randy for the morning. She wanted to get her day started. "I'm really okay. Just taking some 'me' time. I may see some of the girls tonight." She lied.

"Oh, that's great." Randy seemed relieved. "I was just talking to Flora about you. You know she's missed you, right?"

Tabby shuddered. Flora had been a friend Tabby had made from day-care activities. Flora Englewood's daughter was Riley's age. Their only real connection had been their daughters. If Tabby saw Flora, she was certain she'd burst into tears.

Flora had been there the first few weeks following Riley's vanishing. She was just another reminder of the worst days of Tabby's life.

Why was Randy even talking to her?

Tabby didn't care. She just nodded and said: "Yeah, well... I'm thinking of getting some girlfriends from church over."

"Oh, sure. Well, either way I think that's a good thing."

Glad you approve, Randy. "Thanks, hun." Tabby said. "Anything else you need?"

"No. Just wanted to check on you."

"Okay. Well, I'll talk to you later, okay?"

"Okay."

"Okay."

It seemed to be the most prominent word in their vocabulary. As Tabby hung up, she tried to remember the last time they had said "I love you" to one another. Had it been before or after their last struggle to copulate? Making love had been Tabby's idea. She needed to try something to take her mind away from the daily horrors they faced. But it had all ended in tears. Even fucking was just a reminder of the act that had brought Riley into the world in the first place.

Tabby felt her breath waver. Was she really going to start her Friday in tears? Apparently so. It was too late now, and the waterworks were doing their unstoppable thing.

Maybe she'd actually try and invite some old friends over. If anything, she did need to attempt to do something outside of her monotonous routine.

Chapter Three
Win Stupid Prizes

Irwin was hungry.

It had been three months since the last "game".

Greta had been fun. She had been persuaded to slice her ear off, but after her parents woke up the game was cut short. It had left a sour aftertaste in Irwin's mouth. He could only hope that Daddy had something more *spectacular* in mind for the next round.

Irwin sat in front of his computer monitor. He picked at the gunk building up beneath his fingernails with a paper clip. He had twisted the clip into a sharpened prong and was using its metal end to scoop out piles of white and yellow calk. Dirt, scalp particles, boogers, and smegma... it all built up into a sort of "finger-cheese".

He pried it out and then frisked it down his throat with a nimble tongue. He thought it was a better move than just tossing it on the floor. In this way, Irwin saw himself as "well groomed".

Irwin was anything but.

At thirty-eight, he looked well into his fifties. He was morbidly obese. His scalp was balding and prickled with scabs. His face was decorated in acne scars and freshly milked pimples. He wore glasses and rarely shaved. Instead of a full beard, Irwin had only been able to grow a scraggly thatch of pubic hair out from between the folds of his chins. Some of the hairs had become grossly ingrown and the skin around their roots was pink and pus-clogged.

Irwin Monk was also a smelly bastard.

An acerbic odor akin to expired milk hung around him. It was the fungal growths blooming between his unwashed flabs that caused such a stench. He secreted a creamy confection of mossy droplets and sweaty polyps. To any that had the misfortune of seeing and smelling him, Irwin was a living illness. A cancer in human form.

And—believe it or not—he was proud of it.

He loved being gross. He couldn't think of any better state for a person with his fixations.

Irwin sat in front of three computer monitors. One screen was playing muted vomit porn. An Asian woman had her fingers down her mouth and was *heaving* into a funnel, which was piped down another woman's esophagus. They were both teary eyed, but they tried to smile at the camera between waves of upchuck. Honestly, the smiles ruined the whole thing for Irwin. He had stopped cranking his cock, but he let the video play anyways in case it ever got good.

The middle screen was abuzz with messages. He was currently engaged in a discussion on the "DADDY TORTURE-FUCK" forum. They were going over the highlights of the last few games. Gifs of Greta Hilligloss wiping her butt with a bible page were spreading like covid. People seemed to like that, not because of what she was doing... but because of how humiliated she looked while she did it. It was "tasty", according to the members of the forum.

Irwin thought it was kind of weak.

The guy that had been persuaded to pop a stranger's baby in a microwave had been much better.

That was on his second screen. A collage of pictures, gifs, and videos taken from the last few games. And they were glorious.

A woman fucking herself with a dragon-dildo in the middle of a fancy restaurant, much to the shock and horror of the diners.

A child pushing his younger brother's stroller onto a train track at the behest of the cellphone he held between his head and his uplifted shoulder. Irwin remembered exactly what Daddy had said to that boy.

"If you don't do it, I'll kill your mommy and daddy, and I'll make you watch!"

The weeping child's performance had made Irwin shiver with joy.

There was the woman that had sodomized her

brother with a cucumber at gunpoint, apologizing the whole time while Daddy spoke in her ear-piece.

There was the man standing on the edge of a sky-scraper's roof, nude and with a piano wire tied around his cock. He was crying into the phone: "I don't *wanna* do it!"

But he did... they all did. Unless, of course, someone stopped them. An act of God or a nosy passerby.

Irwin had become addicted to the game in its early days. Back then, Daddy had called on people to do simple things.

"Try and steal from your neighbors."

"Record yourself licking a public toilet."

"Piss on a cop car."

Things like that.

In fact, Daddy hadn't even needed to host his show in the dark web. It was out there for everyone and anyone to find. He just called random people and promised them money as long as they completed a few outrageous tasks. It was like your typical prank show. But then, things took a turn. His requests grew darker and meaner... and he found a true fan-base among degenerates like Irwin.

Now, Daddy's message boards were by invitation only, and the things he had people do were... terrible.

The more heinous, the more destructive... the

more exciting to his loyal followers. It was also better financially, Irwin was sure. Sometimes, to get access to the footage Daddy's "contestants" sent in, you had to pay a fee. The amount of crypto currency Irwin had spent on exclusive photos and videos of suffering, humiliation, and degradation was... ghastly. But it didn't bother Irwin.

Irwin, despite his appearances, was rich. He had inherited his fortune from a deceased grandfather, and now he was set up for life. He could afford to sit in his computer room—his lair—and spend money on whatever he saw fit.

A notice appeared on the message board.

DADDY TORTURE-FUCK: *Hey, scum! You all ready for a new game?*

Before anyone else could, Irwin responded enthusiastically.

ARMANDRUMBLE69: *Absolotlee.*

Irwin smiled.

This was how it worked:

Daddy would come into the message board and use their suggestions to pick what tasks he'd ask of their poor contestant.

Last time, it had been Irwin's idea to make the contestant use a cheese-grater on her clit. Of course, they hadn't gotten that far. The phone was wrestled out of Greta's arms by her dad.

So instead, Irwin had been forced to masturbate to the video of Daddy firing a hard load into Donnie Hilligloss. *And not the type of "load" Irwin usually put in a crumpled-up tissue.*

Daddy always compensated his audience. If he had to kill the "prize", they'd get the footage. They'd also get to watch as he dunked the body in a vat of acid and let it deteriorate before it was poured into a grimy bathtub and washed down the drain. His body-disposal method was as efficient as it was grisly.

DADDY TORTURE-FUCK: *Okay, children. What should we do this time?*

Already, perverse suggestions were coming in. Irwin read them with sweaty glee. It was like someone had tapped into Joseph Mengele's stream of consciousness. Of course, Daddy wouldn't pick *all* of them. He'd only get the ones which were feasible; apologies to COINSLOT, who suggested that Daddy make someone do a backflip into a pit of alligators. They also wanted to give the contestant a chance to survive, at least until the very end. The last task was always the same, no matter what, and if they didn't make it to that then what was the point?

Still, none of the tasks were easy. They would push the human body and psyche to its absolute limits. Daddy was already picking a few up and putting heart emoji's by them. He was excited by the suggestions, Irwin could tell. He loved it when his disciples got creative.

Irwin's eyes scanned over to his third monitor. He watched as one of the Asian women evacuated her stomach down the funnel.

He was already getting some nasty ideas.

Chapter Four
Making Attempts

Tabby felt like an island.

There was nothing around her.

Just waves.

Just emptiness.

Just the ocean and its secrets.

That wasn't the truth.

She was sitting in the middle of a bar. There were plenty of things and people to look at. But they all blurred together. An intangible mass of sweaty flesh, blabbering mouths, and vapid stares. None of it made any sense to her anymore.

Even her closest friends felt miles away.

Tabby was seated in one of the corner booths at *Beauregard & Volpe's*. This bar the closest thing the small town of Amherst, Missouri, had to a hip-and-happening place. A couple cowboys stood by the pool table, a few couples loitered by the bar, and Tabby and her girlfriends were stationed at the corner booth, eyes open and hungry. It was an unspoken rule that they were all supposed to keep each other faithful to their husbands, but every time they came to

Beauregard & Volpe's they pretended that they were single. Just to relieve their wilder pre-mom days.

No one ever went too far—except Tabby was fairly certain Kate had given the handsome singer from an open mic night a handy under the table. But she couldn't prove it and didn't really care to. This week, pickings were slim... as were her girlfriends. Only two had made it out following Tabby's rushed invitation.

There was Esther. She was tall, sharp-chinned, steely eyed, and black-haired. She reminded Tabby of a supermodel, and she looked out of place no matter where she stood in Amherst. She had two children and had miraculously zero body fat.

Then there was Pauline. Pauline was homely, frizzy-haired, rosy-cheeked, and spoke with an accent thicker than Tabby's. She was wearing "mom jeans" and a plaid button-up. She looked like the perfect square dance partner. Pauline was a mother of six. Any opportunity to get away from the little horde was an opportunity Pauline was grateful for.

It was Friday night. Tabby only had a few more hours of peace before her life was turned upside down...

...but she wasn't feeling peaceful yet. She was still riled from Randy's presumptuous phone call. How dare he act as if he was the bigger person, just by checking in on her after leaving her to her own devises? She couldn't help but wonder if it wasn't a good idea to kill herself. Just so he would be the one to discover her corpse after crawling back home from his parents.

She shook the dark thoughts out of her head and swallowed a shot of whiskey. She sealed her eyes shut and breathed in through her teeth.

"I'm just thankful you called us out." Pauline said, putting a paw against Tabby's shoulder. Tabby smiled and nodded, as if she was healed. As if this was a sign that things were getting better.

"Yes. We've all needed some gal-time, don't you think?" Esther said affluently as she sipped her beer.

"God." Tabby muttered. "Yes." She slammed another shot.

Pauline chuckled and inconspicuously moved the bottle away from her. Always the mother, even when she was miles away from her kids. Tabby couldn't help but cherish her for her concern.

"How's Chuck?" She asked, referencing Pauline's husband. Chuck was a big dweeb. An enthusiastic Cardinals fan with a "man cave" to boot. He and Randy had gotten along well.

"Oh, you know Chuckie. Same as always." Pauline leaned in close so that only her girlfriends could hear, as if anyone in the bar was paying attention to them. "Last week... we tried *roleplaying*."

"Yeesh. Please tell me it had nothing to do with baseball." Esther hissed.

"H-how'd you know?" Pauline's face went white.

Tabby guffawed. She slapped her knees and seethed: "Because he's got a Cardinal tattooed on his chest, Pauline!"

Pauline crossed her arms and pouted. "I don't care. It was still fun."

"Were you the Mascot or... or the batter?" Esther giggled behind her fingers.

"I think she means did you pitch or catch?"

Pauline laughed and poured herself a shot. "You guys are just jealous because my hubby's a hunk."

"Sure." Esther grinned. Esther's husband, Giorgio, was just as gorgeous as she was. A six-foot four giant with olive skin and strong arms, he was the sort of man that made every woman at their church swoon. And he was Godly too. Tabby was certain he would disapprove of their "wifely" discussions at *Beauregard & Volpe's*. But even church girls liked to gab, and what else was there to talk about in Amherst, Missouri, if one wasn't willing to delve into their own sex lives?

Besides, Tabby was sure that God would

forgive them. As she saw it, God owed her.

"Speaking of, I haven't seen Randy at Church these last weeks." Pauline turned toward Tabby with concern. "He's not sick, is he?"

"No." Tabby said. "He's... he's taking a little break. Went to visit his parents."

"Aw. I miss my parents." Esther stared wistfully ahead. Her parents lived in Greece.

"Well, I just hope he's okay. I hope you both are." Suddenly, Pauline reached out and pulled Tabby into one of her momma-bear hugs. Tabby squeezed back, happy to smell her friends sweat and cheap perfume. It felt good, being held. Tabby found herself wishing she could bare her soul to these wonderful ladies.

But her tongue was tied.

"Thanks." Tabby said as they split apart. She turned and hugged Esther, who was so skinny it was like holding onto a sapling.

Afterwards, the three women sighed and seemed to melt together into a boozy haze. A few drinks later and they were talking animatedly about the things Christian women cared so deeply about. Who was hosting next week's potluck? Was Bible study going to be postponed for the football game? Did any of Pauline's boy's make the team? How were everyone's parents? Had that new yoga place opened yet and were memberships cheap?

Then, a voice broke through their dome of

conversation.

"Excuse me? Is one of you Tabitha Moss?" It was one of the bartenders. A woman with a round face and short hair.

"That's me?" Tabitha raised her hand, as if she was a schoolchild. A thousand thoughts flew through her at once. Was it Randy calling with an emergency? Was Brubaker looking for her? Had a new lead been found in Riley's case? Had her body been found? Trepidation ensnared her.

"We've got a call for you at the bar. Some guy named Irwin?"

"Oh." She didn't recognize the name. She looked back and forth from her girlfriends to the bartender. No one seemed to know what to say.

Esther scooted out so Tabitha could leave the booth. As she followed the bartender, they walked by the cowboys at the pool table. One of the cowboys looked up at her and grinned. She couldn't help but notice how clean his teeth were and how soft his lips looked. He kind of reminded her of the boys on the fronts of those awful romance novels she often perused curiously through at the grocery store.

Tabitha smiled back.

The cowboy turned to his game but kept his eyes on her as she walked by.

At the bar, a red telephone waited for her.

She picked it up nervously and held it to her ear.

"Hello?" Tabitha asked.

"H-hello?" A small and squeaky voice came through.

"Yes. Hello. This is Tabby."

"Tabby? You go by... Tabby?"

"Yes. Who is this?" She impatiently thrummed her fingers against the bar-top. "Forgive me but, I don't think I know an Irwin."

"I just wanted to hear your voice... so I'd know you're real." The little voice snickered.

What a weird thing to say. Tabby furrowed her brow and looked back toward her girlfriends. They were watching with concern. She shrugged and mouthed: "I don't know".

"Well, Tabby... I just wanted to say: 'Good luck'."

"Who are you?" Tabby asked.

"And I'm so looking forward to... *everything*."

"I don't know who you are, dude." Tabby said.

"I'm... I'm just a fan."

Tabby put her hand against her brow and sighed loudly. She didn't like playing these games. "Just tell me who you are."

"You don't know me." Irwin wheezed. "But I just wanted to hear your voice. So that... you know... it'd all be *real*."

"You aren't making any sense. I'm hanging up."

"Wait!" Irwin hissed.

Tabby found herself frozen. She cranked an

eyebrow up and hesitated. On the other end of the line, she could hear something shuffling around. Then, much to her horror, she heard a wet noise. The all too familiar and grisly sound of skin rubbing against skin.

Was he... jerking off?

The line went dead. Tabby shuddered and pulled the phone back, looking at it as if it had transformed into a wriggling sea cucumber. Before going back to her seat, she ordered a glass of beer. It was given to her quickly.

"Who was it?" Esther asked.

"Some weirdo. Said he was a 'big fan'." Tabby frowned as she took a seat beside Pauline. She decided not to tell her girlfriend about the obscene sounds Irwin had made.

Pauline sighed and looked over toward the cowboys lustily. She didn't seem too interested in Tabby's phone-drama. But Esther leaned over and whispered: "I used to get crank calls from some creep."

"Yeah?" Tabby asked.

"It got so bad we had to call the police. He'd call every night right after we put the kids to bed."

"You'd think that wouldn't be a big deal anymore with caller ID."

"They can mask their ID's nowadays." Esther shrugged. "Anything is possible."

"Did you ever find out who it was?"

Esther shivered. "No. One day he just stopped calling."

"What did he say?" Pauline was back.

"When he called?" Esther frowned. "You don't want to know. The grossest stuff you've ever heard. To this day I refuse to pick up the phone for unknown numbers."

Tabby looked back toward the bar. Maybe she should have taken the creep's number down. Maybe she should have let the bartender know it was a weird call. Maybe... maybe... it was all too distant now and she didn't really want to worry about it. Still, the name of her caller stuck in her head. Irwin. Was that his real name or a pseudonym?

Tabby didn't want to know. She cleared her mind and re-focused on her beer.

Chapter Five
Surveillance

The video was of Greta. She was sitting with her hands on her lap and her head held high. Her ear was a frayed flap of skin, healed but damaged beyond repair. She'd never look "normal" again. Daddy pressed "play" and listened to her talk.

"The man who did this to me is a coward that hides behind anonymity. We have no idea who he is, or what became of my husband... but what he did is... unforgivable."

Daddy smiled. His lips pulled over his sharp teeth. His tongue flicked out like a lizard. He loved hearing them rationalize everything they had been through. Greta had been something of a disappointment as far as games went. They hadn't even made it to the second task before she was interrupted.

But this next one... it was going to be different.

Daddy had a lot of great tasks planned and he was certain that the contestant would be a noble one.

The interviewer was asking Greta more questions about her day-to-day life now that she had survived such a harrowing ordeal. Her story was going to be used as the inspiration for an upcoming episode of a popular cop show. The program was focused on internet predators. A documentary had already been made about what had happened, and she was in talks with a major publishing company to write a book about that fateful morning.

As far as Daddy was concerned, Greta Hilligloss should be thanking him.

He made a mental note to pick up the book when it was out.

Daddy returned to his primary tab. On it was a picture of Tabitha Gilman Moss. She was holding her baby close to her chest. She was all smiles, totally unaware that her child was going to be taken from her. Totally unaware that it all led up to tomorrow morning. All of the trauma, the grief, the pain, and the loss. It would be realized the second she woke up.

Daddy wasn't a coward. Greta had it all wrong. He liked to be close to the action. He didn't make the calls from a million miles away or from the safety of his basement.

No.

He was *here*.

In Amherst.

Stationed in the back of what had once been a weather van, his computer monitor illuminated a playground of take-out boxes, weaponry, and a burlap sack. The sack was curled up beneath Daddy's feet. It had cost a pretty penny, but the donations would more than make up for it. Daddy knew it was worth it the moment he saw Tabitha's story on the internet.

What better contestant than a mother? She'll do anything to see her baby returned to her. Anything…

She'd even thank Daddy by the time this was over. Even though she'd be bleeding, broken, and less than human… she'd fall down at his feet and give him thanks. Because unlike the police, her friends, and her deadbeat husband… Daddy had brought Riley home.

And all it had taken was a winning bid on an illegal auction site. It was surprising to him just how cheap children were, relatively.

The sack shuddered.

Daddy kicked it and it squealed.

"Shhh, hun." Daddy rasped. "Mommy's close."

The girl whimpered like a submissive puppy.

"Hey, boss." Markos spoke up from the front seat.

Daddy removed his headphones and gazed up at his accomplice. Markos looked like the heavy from an eighties action movie. With a narrow mullet, an overlarge chin, bright red cheeks, and acne scars. Despite his strength, he was no ladies-man. Markos had long, yellowed nails too. No matter how much shit Daddy gave him, he was never willing to trim. Or even groom.

Being associated with Markos had its ups and downs. The dude was tough as nails and didn't mind getting his paws dirty. He was bodyguard, servant, and brawn. When Daddy needed a limb hacked away, Markos was happy to comply. In fact, the brute didn't even take a salary. He did it because he loved it. Sure, he accepted lodging at Daddy's manor—and the affluence afforded to him. But he truly valued his work. It was a rare thing, finding a man willing to chop the limbs away from a six-year-old.

But Daddy couldn't help but complain about the stench Markos carried. All the mess around their van was Markos's doing. He also refused to put on deodorant, so he smelled like a zoo.

But, again, his work spoke up for his lesser qualities.

Daddy, on the other hand, was clean shaven. He smelled of expensive cologne and minty toothpaste. His black hair was cut long, and his skin was tanned. He didn't look like the type of guy that spent a majority of his time harassing people online, but that was just how he liked it. No one suspected the trust-fund kid until they were caught red handed.

Daddy Torture-Fuck was only twenty-five years old. Markos was thirty.

"What's up?" Daddy asked.

"She's headed out."

Daddy crawled up to the passenger seat and squinted through the tinted glass. A trio of women exited *Beauregard & Volpe's* in high spirits. Tabitha was at the end of the group. Her blonde hair was pulled so far back he imagined her scalp snapping loose. She was carrying a half-full bottle of beer and her steps were wobbly. Daddy checked his digital wristwatch. It was only eight and these women were already sloshed.

Markos licked his lips. Daddy knew exactly what he wanted. He wanted to take one of the extra women and kill her, just for the hell of it. But he'd have to simmer down and focus that energy on the game. That's why Daddy was the brains of the operation. If left up to Markos, the game would simply be a massacre.

Daddy opened his phone and looked at the forum. It was ablaze. Irwin had won the "first call" bidding and had recorded himself harassing Tabitha. It was exciting stuff. Daddy wondered if Irwin was fit at all. If he was, he may make a good third to their crew.

At the very least, he was a loyal follower.

Daddy took his phone and snapped a quick picture of the women walking toward their respective cars. He zoomed in on Tabitha and added a line of white text over her face:

"In Amherst".

He sent it to the chat. The followers began to

swarm around the picture like insects about a crumb.

ARMANDRUMBLE69: So excited!

COINSLOT: Omg she's hot

BRAYER5: Make her suffer!

FREEKEE666: Where is Amherst? New England?

Daddy sat back with a smile.

They watched as Tabby said goodbye to her friends. As they parted ways, she looked back toward the bar... longingly. It made sense. She was living by herself in a child-less and husband-less home. She wouldn't be hurrying back anytime soon. But her girlfriends had husbands and kids aplenty between them... they had responsibilities.

From the back of the van, the abducted child stirred. Her hands and ankles were zip-tied together, and she had a length of duct-tape wrapped around her mouth. She was wearing a diaper and she had been chemically blinded. Someone had poured bleach into her poor eyes. Daddy wished he had been there to watch it happen. Or at least he wished her assailant had had the good graces to record the blinding. Videos of children being tortured made a pretty penny on the market.

"Get your camera, Markos." Daddy instructed. "We're gonna go ahead and take the picture."

Markos reached into the glove compartment

and pulled out his Polaroid camera. He giggled, as if he had gotten exactly what he wanted for Christmas.

Daddy put his hand out on Markos's shoulder and gripped it.

"Wait a moment, buddy. I've got an idea..."

He looked out the window and watched as Esther separated from the group.

Chapter Six
Every Parent's Worst Nightmare

Esther wasn't so certain she should be driving home. She was a little closer to drunk than buzzed.

She pulled out her phone and rang her husband. Giorgio picked up quickly.

"Yes, my love?" He asked in a warm tone.

"Can you get me from *Beauregard & Volpe's*?" She asked calmly. "You're wife made a boo-boo."

Giorgio laughed. "The kids are just getting ready for bed. Give me a few, okay?"

Their children were both in their tweens and didn't mind being left home alone every once in a while. They were smart and knew their parent's numbers, so there was no reason to worry about them. Still, Esther couldn't help but feel a lingering sense of dread crawl up her spine. Maybe that happened whenever she was around Tabitha. Poor Tabby had gone through the worst thing imaginable for a parent. Losing either of her children was a possibility, but it was one Esther didn't like to focus on.

She knew that God would protect her babies.

"I love you, sweetie." She cooed into her

phone.

"I love you too, honey-bee." Giorgio laughed. "Are you too drunk for a little husband-wife time tonight?"

Esther hissed with laughter, recalling Pauline's role-playing story. "I'm never too drunk for *that*." She muttered.

Speak of the devil, and she shall drive by and flash her lights. Pauline beeped the horn before her car rushed out from the lot and careened down the highway. Pauline was certainly too drunk to be on the road but didn't have the wherewithal to call her hubby.

With six young ones, Esther didn't imagine Chuck could pull himself away from home to pick up his inebriated wife.

"I'll see you soon." Giorgio said.

"*Byyyye*." Esther imitated a valley-girl. They laughed as they hung up. Esther leaned against her car and put her palm against her brow, as if she was testing for a fever.

"Hey."

"Whoa!" Esther whirled around, frightened by the sudden presence on the other side of her car.

The young man held up his hands defensively. "Sorry! Sorry! Didn't mean to scare you." He grinned sheepishly.

"Sorry." Esther laughed and held her hand over her mouth. "You just startled me."

"I should've not done that." The boy giggled. His voice was softer than Esther had expected. He called to mind the image of a cowboy poet rather than a gunslinger. "I just wanted to check on you. You looked a little concerned there."

"No. It's fine. I just called my husband; he's picking me up."

"Oh." He was obviously disappointed to learn she was married. He pocketed his hands and kicked at the gravel beneath his feet. "I just figured you may need a jump or a ride or something. My bad."

"Thank you." Esther beamed. "I appreciate it." She recognized him now. He was one of the cowboy's from the bar. The one that hadn't been able to keep his eyes off Tabby as she walked by to receive that weird phone call.

"Are you... sorry if this is forward... are you looking for someone tonight?" Esther asked.

The cowboy shrugged. "Shucks. Is it obvious?"

"Do you want to know what you should do?"

He frowned.

"My friend Tabby—you saw her. She's going through a rough time and... things are rocky with her husband. She won't say it but, they're separated." Was she actually suggesting this? Maybe it was because she was drunk, but she felt like being a naughty ambassador. "I can't make you any promises, but you should try your luck with her."

"Yeah?" The cowboy reached behind his head and scratched his curly hair. "Thanks, hun."

"No problem. I could give you her number if—"

Esther's face fell when she saw the figure appear behind the cowboy. At first, she thought she was hallucinating. But the slender man wearing a white mask was no dream. He was wearing a black duster and his hands were gloved in leather. His mask was almost featureless except for its vacant eye-holes. Behind them, his pupils conveyed fury. The nose and mouth were smooth, but the cheeks were well-sculpted and handsome. He wore a hairnet, and his throat was so clean shaven, it looked ivory.

There was a flash of motion, and she saw that he was armed. A hunting knife gripped in his right hand imbedded itself into the base of the cowboy's back. The assailant drew it out as quickly as he had put it in. It was followed by a gust of crimson blood and a shriek.

The cowboy turned around, leaning his back against Esther's passenger door. He held his hands up and watched helplessly as the assailant attacked with a flurry of stabs. The knife cut through the middle of his right palm, spraying blood across the cowboy's face, and filling his mouth.

"No!" The cowboy said.

The knife flashed forward and dug into his

clavicle. Its steel body swept in and out like a lizard's tongue frisking the air for flies. Two more stabs, and the cowboy's neck was gushing blood and oozing cartilage. The white pipe of his esophagus was exposed to the chilly night's air.

Esther watched without a sound. It didn't seem real. One second, she was engaging in pleasantries... the next, a man was being killed right in front of her.

The cowboy fell over and landed on the hood of her car. His blood trickled down toward the grill. He struggled in place, worming about as if he was drunk. The killer stabbed him in the belly. The blade cut through a layer of fat and came out with a hiss. Blood squirted up and decorated the killer's duster.

The fiend continued to stab, his knife working quickly. The cowboy had been stabbed nine times now. Once in the back, once in the palm, once in the clavicle, twice in the throat, and now four times in the stomach. The tenth stab was aimed more for his pelvis. It landed right on his pubic mound and cracked through his pelvic bone with a sickening *smack*.

The killer ground the blade in, twisting and turning as if he was digging for treasure.

Esther took a step back and collided with a massive figure.

She turned and was frightened to see a secondary white mask, identical to the first. Only this brute was less well-dressed. He was wearing a grey tank-top and a pair of sweatpants. She saw, much to her terror, that he wasn't wearing underpants. His erection was firm.

He gripped her by the throat, canceling her intended screams. He wrestled her around so that she was forced to watch as the cowboy was killed.

His cries had turned into airy wheezes. The killer had stepped back and was wiping the blood away from his eye-holes with a gloved hand. The killer whirled his arm through the air and planted the knife in the pit that had once been the cowboy's belly. Esther saw a coiled rope of purple intestine come loose and wriggle out from his cavity. It slapped against the hood of her car before unfurling and dangling past the grill.

The killer pulled the knife free and took a deep breath, as if he had just stepped away from an elliptical.

"She was on the phone with someone." The killer said, panting for breath. "We have to be fast."

"But..." The giant holding her throat whined.

"No buts. We gotta be fast."

"But what if we take her away from here?"

The killer shook his head. "We'll get you one you can play with later. I promise, Markos. Just do it. Now."

The giant grunted with anger. He put a massive paw on the back of Esther's head... and slammed her face into the side of her car. She felt her nose shatter and watched as a white bone popped out just beneath her eyeline. It was followed by slurry of blood and flesh-pulp.

The brute thumped her into the car again, mashing her face into the window. It didn't break the way they did in movies. Instead, her face was forced to rupture. A large gash opened up across her left cheek and blood fanned out across the window. It even leaked into the seal.

The man pulled her away and dropped her to the ground.

Esther took in a lungful of hot air. She followed it up with a volley of coughs. Her fists began to close over the gravel beneath her. She squirmed in slow strides.

A knee collided with her back, pinning her to the ground.

"Gimme the knife, boss." The giant growled.

She heard the exchange, but didn't exactly comprehend it—

—until the blade was at her throat.

There was no hesitation. The giant see-sawed the blade across her white throat, opening a yawning mouth beneath her chin. Red liquid sprayed out, hissing as it came unleashed from her. The blade had severed the carotid artery and the juggler in a few easy turns.

It was now biting into her esophageal wall.

Esther felt vomit travel up her chest and through her throat. Only it never made it to her mouth. A mix of yellow beer and half-digested French fries spluttered out of her secondary orifice. It was followed by another eruption of blood and slimy bile.

No, Jesus, please, Jesus... I'm sorry, Jesus. Let me live. I don't want to die. I just want to go home. Please, let Giorgio find me right now. Please. Please. Please.

The blade had cut to the base of her white spinal cord. The giant stabbed the knife into the ground and affixed both of his hands around the edges of her wound. In one mad jerk, he pulled her head back, snapping it so that it lay between her shoulder blades. He reached into the mess that had been her throat and grabbed ahold of her spinal cord. With angry grunts, he began to decapitate her by hand.

With a meaty twist and a hard yank, Esther's head came away from her shoulders. It was followed by another splattering of strawberry textured fluids. Her hair was so greased with blood, it looked bright scarlet. Her busted cheek was leaking, and mucus was squeezing its way out of her nostrils, like green caterpillars.

Markos stood and held the head up for Daddy Torture-Fuck to observe.

"Good job, buddy." His masked leader said as

he stooped over to retrieve the hunting knife. "Shove the body underneath the car. I'll take that."

He took the head from Markos's hands and wandered back toward the van.

Markos looked down at Esther's headless corpse. He grinned as he hefted it up and rolled it beneath the car. Even on short notice, he had still made her hurt. Her cries and whimpers and the spraying of her bodily fluids would be enough fuel for tonight's spank bank.

He hesitated before pushing her all the way beneath the car. Tentatively, he touched her rear, and was happy to find it filled. She, like most of his victims, had evacuated her bowels as she died.

If only there had been more time.

Markos sighed and finished the job.

He took a handful of the cowboy's shirt and yanked him from the hood. He left a slug's trail of blood in his wake. A tender stripe of entrails clung to the grill as the cowboy was shoved under the car and beside Esther's corpse.

The two made for good bedfellows, Markos thought with a cheery grin.

As he stood up, he heard a shuffling stampede of footsteps.

He turned around, knife upraised.

Marko was relieved to see his boss running up to his side.

"Wait!" Daddy gasped between mouthfuls of air. "Wait! I just got the sickest idea *ever*. Pull the dude out."

Markos didn't mind exhuming the cowboy from his gravelly grave. If his boss had a spur-of-the-moment idea, Markos was certain it was something no one would soon forget.

Chapter Seven
Empty Home

Tabby flicked the light on in her bedroom and released a long and discontented sigh.

After spending a few hours with Pauline and Esther, Tabby didn't really want to be alone right now.

She wondered if God would have forgiven her if she had sought solace in the arms of one of the cowboys at the pool table. At least one of them had looked fairly handsome.

She sighed again, knowing she'd been asking her Lord and Savior a few hypotheticals too many.

Still, she felt she was owed.

Her house was empty. It was a crushed beer can. It was haunted by nothingness. It was vacant and hollow.

Even now, she strove to hear Riley's animated footsteps in her room. Riley had a habit of waking up at odd hours in the night and pacing from one corner of her room to the other. Randy had supposed she was naturally nocturnal and would wind up living most of her life at night if allowed. Tabby had been concerned that it would make school scheduling a living hell for her little angel.

Tabby groaned, shucking away her clothes and lying face-first on her bed. The room was chilly, but she didn't have the strength to wrap herself up in her blanket. Instead, she reached up and pulled her hair loose. A curtain of dusty blonde follicles fell over her cheeks and tickled her eyelids.

You have to stop thinking about Riley. She's gone. She's gone.

It was impossible for her to do so.

Riley was everywhere.

Every single thing Tabby encountered traced back to her missing daughter.

She just couldn't help but ponder over what had become of her.

Maybe she's safe. Maybe she lost her memory and is with a different family now. Maybe they'll take care of her.

Maybe she's been harvested for her little organs. Oh, god, her pancreas.... Her liver... oh god...

Tabby buried her head into her bed. She sniffed in the scent of her clean sheets and tried to focus on that. It grounded her for a brief period of time. Enough so that she could grab ahold of her brain and steer it a different direction.

She thought of the night she had just shared

with her pals from church. It really had been good to reconnect with them. And aside from a few schmaltzy moments, it had never felt too forced or unearned.

Tabby felt as if she was making real progress to be a human being again.

Maybe, someday, she'd come home, and she wouldn't be burdened with guilt and pain.

She turned her head. Eyes closed, face quilted in hair, she tried to sleep through force of will. The beers and shots she'd enjoyed were now burning in her stomach. Her blood felt like sludge in her veins. It was the perfect combination of heaviness that aided in her drowsiness.

In no time at all, Tabby was asleep.

In her dreams… she saw Riley.

Her little girl was in hell and surrounded by demons. They lashed at her body with fearsome whips made out of spinal cords and tipped with shattered glass. They clawed at her skin, pulling it away from her musculature in meaty handfuls.

All around her, there was fire.

The flames peeled away her flesh and exposed the white bones beneath.

Above her, Tabby was lashed to the stone ceiling. Her arms and legs were immobile, but her head seemed to be free. She shook it back and forth and screamed:

"Leave her alone! You bastards! Leave her alone!"

The demons, red-skinned and horned, looked up at her with toothy grins. They had no intention of letting either of them free.

From the corner of the demonic cathedral, Randy spoke up. He had been melted down into a pile of polyps and shuddering warts. His voice was slurred and wet. "I think we just need space... to forget."

A demon stepped on him. It was like watching a shoe crush a mound of dog-shit.

Her husband squeezed out along the sides of the demon's bare foot.

His gunk zipped up between the monster's wriggling toes.

"Momma!" Riley cried as a demon took her scalp and began to yank it away from her skull. Her face was a red skeleton. All bone and strands of blackened vein. Blood oozed out of her crying mouth and dribbled down her front. "Momma! Why can't you save me?"

"I'm sorry!" Tabitha cried. "I'm so... so... sorry!"

Tabitha awoke with a sudden gasp. The nightmare dissipated around her, and she was returned to her empty bedroom. Naked, sprinkled in sweat and breathing heavily... she had never had a dream so bad. Even at the height of their search for Riley, her sleep had been to exhausted and short for nightmares.

But this one had felt so real, even though the finer details were washing away now... like scum down a drain.

Tabitha covered her eyes and began to weep.

Part Two
Guts

Chapter Eight
Grisly Games

Tabby noticed the brown bag sitting on her front porch the moment she opened the door. She was fully dressed in jeans and a button up. The morning air was frigid, and she was ready to go out and grab her Saturday morning paper.

She hadn't been expecting a deviation from her usual ritual. The paper lunch bag threw her off.

Tabby stooped over and picked the item up. It wasn't all that heavy, but it definitely wasn't empty. Tabitha brought it inside, closing the door behind her. The paper could wait.

She set the bag down and took a seat at the dining room table. She ran her fingers through her hair before unfurling the bag and dumping loose its contents.

Out came a black cellphone.

When it hit the table, its screen lit up. The display screen was not customized. It looked like a fresh model, right off the rack.

Tabitha shook the bag and watched as a Polaroid picture fell out. Her heart filled with dread the moment she looked at the picture.

No... it can't be... it can't...

Tabitha picked the picture up and examined it with shaky fingers. It struck terror and revulsion in her heart. She felt yesterday's drinks rising up her throat. She put a hand against her mouth and held her heaves back.

Jesus Christ.

Riley was in the picture.

There was no doubt in Tabby's mind. It was her little girl. Her hair was greasy and unwashed. It had also grown past her shoulders. She was wearing a pink shirt that Tabby didn't recognize. But it was her.

Something was wrong with her eyes. They were scabrous and sealed shut. Gummy pus seemed to be welling up between her lids.

Her skin was pale and looked spongy in the dim light of the Polaroid.

There was a human head sitting on her lap. It was bloated with bruises and the hair was sticky with coagulated blood. But Tabby knew it was Esther's head. She recognized her, despite her injuries.

Jesus Christ. Tabby thought with dread.

She turned the picture over and found a note written in red marker:

No cops. Wait for our call.

Tabby set the picture down on the table and covered her mouth with both hands. She still felt as if she was trapped in her horrible dreams from the previous night. Only this was undeniably real. Or... was it? Tabby fully expected to jerk awake again, the way she had last night. She expected to find herself tangled up in her sweaty sheets, crying out to an empty room. But there was no reprieve. She was stuck here in her dining room, confronting a picture of her mutilated and abused child.

Oh, God. What did they do to her eyes?

Tabby's fear was quickly being replaced with anger. White hot fury drilled itself into her ribcage and sat down on her heart. Its pressure was immense.

They hurt her. They hurt your baby. Oh, Jesus. They hurt your baby girl and you couldn't do a thing to stop them.

Tabby's eyes went from white to red. She imagined driving a hammer into the head of the sick photographer. She imagined lassoing him and stringing him up from one of the trees on her farm. She imagined putting them through whatever hell Riley had been through.

But there was nothing she could do. And that was the worst of it.

She had to sit and wait for their call.

No cops.

What use had the cops been anyways? She remembered when Riley had gone missing; she was talking to the detective in charge of her case. A stout man named Matt Brubaker. Brubaker had reassured her as she sobbed:

"Riley is top priority for me and our department. I promise you, ma'am, we'll find her."

She had clung to that promise. In her greatest moments of despair, she would think, *Brubaker promised he'd find her. He promised.*

She had trusted Brubaker. He was small, strong, and spoke in a sweet tone. When she yelled at him, he took it with the grace of Christ. He was gentle to her when she needed it, and firm when he had to be.

"We're doing our best."

"We're working around the clock."

"No new leads today, ma'am. But tomorrow looks promising."

"We'll find her. We will."

But Brubaker hadn't found her.

Instead, Tabitha had woke up on an unassuming Saturday, and had been delivered what had to be a ransom letter. Well, whatever those sick bastards wanted, she'd pay. She'd give anything to see Riley again. Anything.

Anything.

Then the rest of the image hit her. Esther's decapitated head. Whoever had stolen Riley must have been at the bar yesterday. Or at least, they had been watching Tabby. She recalled the bizarre phone call she had received. The obscene one from Irwin.

Was Irwin the abductor?

And why had they killed Esther? Just to show how fresh the photo was? Or just to prove that they were fucked up? They didn't need to prove themselves. The very fact that they were holding her six-year-old daughter hostage—and had blinded her—was enough.

"I'll kill you." Tabby seethed through her teeth. "I'll find you and I'll fucking kill you." It was a promise she hoped to keep, unlike the ones Brubaker espoused.

The phone rang.

Tabby answered it quickly. Snapping with vehemence, she belted into the phone: "Who *the fuck* are you?"

The other end of the line was silent. Dead silent. She could hear breathing, but her caller was in no rush.

"Hello?" Tabby growled. "Where's my daughter? Where is she you *fuck*??"

The line went dead. They had hung up.

Tabby was mortified. She recoiled and stared at the blank screen on the phone. Her eyes drifted back to the Polaroid. Back to Riley. Had she already failed her little girl by insulting her kidnappers?

Tabby felt a wave of shame and regret cascade over her.

When the phone rang again, she answered with a gasp of relief, as if she had just broken through the surface after a drowning scare.

Tears streamed down her face. She didn't speak. She didn't dare speak.

"Hello, Tabitha." The voice on the other end was slick and greasy. It reminded her of a radio DJ. The type that thought the epitome of humor was delivering unfortunate news with a smile.

"Hello." She responded, her voice a whimper of its former self.

"Are you ready to listen?"

"Yes." Tabby confirmed. "I'll pay anything—"

"I know." The man seethed. "I know you'll pay anything. But I want to know if you'll *do* anything."

Tabby sucked in her lips and squeezed her eyes shut. Her body felt like a washing machine; all swirly and soaked. Sweat poured out beneath her arms and behind her knees. Her right leg jerked uncontrollably.

"How far will you go to save your daughter, Tabitha?" The man seemed to be languishing in his dominance. He was the master, and she was a dog on a leash. Already, he owned her. Just by showing her the picture he held dominion over her.

She wished she knew what he looked like just so she knew who to hate.

"What do you want?" Tabby asked.

"I want to play a game with you, Tabitha." He kept repeating her name, as if it was a magic spell. As if he could hypnotize her. "It's simple...

you play along, and Riley lives. You don't... and... well." He left it at that.

"You have to let her go." Tabby started to plead. "She's just a little girl. Please—"

"Either I give her to you with or without her limbs." He stated his ultimatum bluntly.

"What?" Tabby asked.

"If you say 'without', then we cut corners. My associate and I will amputate Riley's limbs. All four of them. Her legs and her arms. You'll get her back, but she'll be about as useful as a fucking maggot."

The image was as strong as a nightmare.

She imagined this cruel man and his unpleasant assistant taking a hacksaw to her daughter. She wondered if Riley would even survive such a procedure.

"Or... we play a game. And each round you win is another limb spared." He let his words sink in. "You'll get Riley back just the way you last saw her... sans eyes, of course. And I do apologize. That wasn't my doing."

As if this twisted fiend was above blinding a child after having threatened to cut her arms and legs away.

What choice did Tabby have in this matter?

She could have Riley delivered to her in hours, only after having suffered more torment than a child should be forced to bear.

Or she could play along.

The choice was obvious.

"I'll play." Tabby spat. "Please. Let's play. Just you and me, okay? Don't touch my baby girl. Please."

"You don't even know the rules." The man laughed. "You don't even know what you're signing up for."

"Tell me. What are we playing? Please?"

"It's like Simon Says. And I'm Simon. I'm always Simon."

On the other end, Tabby could hear someone laughing. His voice was low and bestial. It drew to mind images of a warthog.

"I tell you to do something... and you do it. And if you don't, then Riley loses."

Tabby bit into the tip of her tongue.

"Easy-peasy?"

"Yes."

"You gotta say 'lemon-squeezy'."

Tabby nodded viciously. "Lemon-squeezy." She returned.

"Good! You're already getting the hang of it!" The man on the other end paused. "My names not Simon though."

"What is it?" She didn't expect him to give her his actual name. She was certain that someone this diabolical wouldn't be so stupid. But anything she could work with would help. She was disappointed by his answer:

"You can call me Daddy." He laughed.

She realized then that she was speaking to the Devil.

This was no mere pervert, like the loser that had harassed her at the bar.

This wasn't a prank call, or a sick joke.

She was talking to the embodiment of evil.

And he was all that stood between her and a reunion she had been dreaming of for months on end.

Riley, I'll see you... I'll do anything for you. I'll do whatever he says.

Whatever he says.

Chapter Nine
Dry Run

"Are you ready for the first round?" Daddy sneered.

"Yes." Tabby returned.

"You don't sound ready."

"I am! I am! I'm ready." Tabby sat on the edge of her seat, as if she was hoping to be picked by her favorite teacher. "Please, let's play."

"I don't know." Daddy muttered flamboyantly. "Hmm. Maybe we need to try it out first, just to make sure you've got the concept in your empty fucking skull?"

Tabby froze. She didn't want to do anything she didn't *have* to. She didn't want to follow this creepy bastard's instructions if it didn't head directly toward her daughter. But what choice did she have?

"I'm ready." She started to insist.

"No. You're just saying that. You don't understand what we're doing here yet, do you?"

She couldn't lie. "No."

"I thought not."

"I don't know what you're capable of or what you want me to do... but... but I'll do anything.

Do you hear me? I'll do *anything*!"

"Then tell your husband you want him to kill himself."

Tabby felt her heart drop. Time seemed to slow, and she waited for Daddy to reveal that it was only a joke. But he had sounded so serious. More serious than he had during the entire duration of their call.

"What?" She asked, dumbfounded.

"That's the practice run. Just to see if you're really a good sport or not. If you can't do this, then you definitely won't play the rest of the game." He paused, taking his time with each word. "And if you don't want to play the game... then I guess you don't want Riley's arms or legs."

The implications were harrowing. She'd be ending her marriage and saving her child's life in one motion. But it was a motion that brought her blood to a standstill in her veins. Her bowels seemed clogged, and her stomach rumbled tersely. She had never said even one cross word to Randy. Even at their worst moments, they had been cordial to each other. She didn't want him to die, and she definitely didn't want him to kill himself.

But he'd understand.

After it was all over, and Riley was returned home, she'd explain to him what had happened. She could tell him the truth, and he'd forgive her. He would even say: "I'd have done the same thing in your shoes." But still, she dreaded having to say it.

"I'm recording you." Daddy said. "Make it sound good."

Tabby turned her head, expecting to find a camera in her dining room with her. Of course, there wasn't one. Unless Daddy had slipped a spy-cam beside a picture frame.

Then, Tabby realized what he meant. He was recording this call. Every word they said would be immortalized.

But to what purpose?

Maybe so he can look back and laugh at all the fun we're having.

She heard a ringing on the other line. Before she could say anything, Randy's voice came through the cellphone. It was muffled by the distance.

"Hello?" Randy asked. "Who's this?"

Daddy didn't say a word. The ball was in Tabby's court now.

What does he expect me to do? Just blurt it out? Or does he want me to talk to him? I wasn't ready. Oh, God, will he hurt Riley if I 'fail'? Tabby's brain was abuzz with worries and scenarios. She licked her dry lips and spoke in a whimper:

"Randy? It's me."

"Oh." Randy said, relieved. "Hi, Tabs. What's

up? New phone?"

"Yeah." Tabby said, not sure if that was a lie or not. What was Daddy doing between their words? Holding back laughter?

"Randy. I have something to say to you." Tabby said.

"Yeah?" He sounded concerned. It broke her heart, knowing that he was worried for her. Knowing that what she was about to say was unforgivable.

Tabby owned two guns. One sat underneath her bed in a locked box and the other was in the glove compartment of her car. She'd never really considered using them on a human being, but now she wondered how many times she'd shoot Daddy before she was satisfied. She imagined devouring his face with bullets.

Even though she didn't know what he looked like, she closed her eyes and imagined seeing the ground through his mulched head.

"What's going on, Tabby?" Randy asked after a beat of silence crossed between them.

"Why didn't you keep your eyes on her?" Tabby spat. Her words were venom. They hadn't blamed each other for Riley's disappearance. At least, not vocally. But now she was dredging it up. All for the amusement of a madman.

"W-what?" Randy asked.

"You weren't watching her. You weren't paying attention... and she was stolen from us."

"It wasn't—" His defense squealed to a stop.

"I hate you, Randy." *God, please make this stop. Let me wake up from this bad dream.* "I hate you."

Randy didn't say anything. He just breathed in heavily.

"I hate you." Tabby repeated with a sob. She couldn't say what Daddy needed her to say. Her voice was breaking, as if she were a boy going through puberty. "I'm... I'm so sorry."

"It's okay." Randy released a gust of air. "Please, Tabby. I'll come home and we can talk about this. We can talk about Riley and... us."

"No." Tabby asserted. "No. I don't want to talk. I want... I want you to..."

"What, Tabby? Anything."

She had to say it. Daddy would kill her daughter if she didn't. She no longer prayed that God would forgive her. She only hoped Randy could.

"I want you to kill yourself."

Silence. Horrible, cloying silence. Tabby wished she would just die. She wished her heart would stop in her chest and she'd be taken away from this terrible day.

She could feel Randy's pain and heartache. He released a sob and said: "What?"

She had to continue. Otherwise, who knew what Daddy would do to Riley? She had to do what she had to do.

"I want you to kill yourself, Randy. Kill yourself. It's the only thing you can do to make this right—"

Daddy hung up on Randy. Before her husband could even process the terrible things Tabby had said. Instantly, Tabby was screaming at her tormentor.

"Fuck you! Fuck you, you piece of shit!"

Daddy laughed. "You better be good to me... or I'll be bad to Riley."

Tabby froze. Her teeth sawed into her tongue, drawing blood. "You son of a bitch." Tabby breathed.

"Oh, I'm worse than that." Daddy laughed. "You passed our practice run. You've convinced me that you want to play."

"Who are you?"

"I'm 'Daddy'."

"No. No. What's your name?" Tabby shook her head. Tears stained her cheeks. "You have to tell me."

"I don't *have* to do anything, Tabitha." Daddy growled. "But you... you *have* to do whatever I tell you to."

Suddenly, a message pinged on the screen. She clicked on it and was shocked to see that Daddy had sent her a picture. On it, Riley was crammed into the back seat of a crowded and messy van. A large muscle-bound man was holding her, as if she was a struggling hog. He had a gun shoved into her little mouth. Its barrel was mashing against her lips, drawing blood. The man was wearing a white mask over his face, but Tabby could see his eyes. They were enlarged with joy.

"Stop!" Tabby stood. "Stop! Don't hurt her!"

"Play the game and she'll be fine."

"We'll play! Let's play! Please!"

"Eager beaver." Daddy cackled. "God, I love hearing you beg!"

Chapter Ten
Toothpicks

Matthew Brubaker was still wracking his brains over it.

Last night, a panicked Giorgio Soavi called the police and begged for help. He had found his wife's headless corpse crammed beneath her vehicle. A sight Brubaker didn't wish on his worst enemies, much less a family man like Giorgio.

As far as Giorgio knew, he had gotten a call from a tipsy Esther; he had driven out to pick her up from the bar, and within the space of his fifteen-minute drive... someone had sawed her head off with a blade. Her throat was decorated in cuts and her blood had fanned across the gravel lot beside her car.

Matthew pinched his brow and wished he could bury his head underneath his pillow and fall asleep. Deaths like this were rare in Amherst.

In fact, they never happened.

The worst Brubaker had seen was a stabbing between irate junkies, a few sloppy shootings, and some gruesome car accidents. He had never seen someone decapitated purposefully.

And whoever had done it had seemed to enjoy making as much of a mess as possible.

Bastard. Sick, twisted bastard. Brubaker thought with a grimace. He couldn't believe just how messed up people could be.

Brubaker was thankful to be stationed in Amherst. Detective work here was rarely trying. Aside from Tabitha Moss's missing child and a few violent disputes, they didn't really have to deal with too much heartache here. Most of Brubaker's job was regulated to paperwork and phone calls. He wasn't used to facing the absolute worst that humanity had to offer. But he saw it in the news. Every day, something horrible was happening. And now... now it was here.

A headless corpse crammed underneath a car.

Giorgio was wrapped in a blanket, like a fuzzy burrito. He was sitting in the back of an ambulance. He had fainted twice since calling in his wife's murder. The paramedics didn't want to take any chances and were getting ready to rush him to the hospital. But Brubaker insisted they share a few words. He needed something to pursue. Anything.

"Giorgio, you have to tell me this... who was Esther meeting?" He asked.

"I don't know." Giorgio rubbed his swollen eyes. He was still sobbing. Brubaker couldn't blame him. "A couple girls from Church."

"Did she tell you any names?"

"I can't... I can't remember." Giorgio sounded like a child.

They went to the same Church. Matthew Brubaker closed his eyes and tried to remember who Esther talked to the most. It was a blur, but he could kind of picture her standing with Pauline early in the morning before services started. "Was it Pauline? Did she come here to meet Pauline?"

If so, maybe Pauline was in danger. Or maybe she had seen something. Something inconspicuous, but helpful. Brubaker needed to know.

Giorgio nodded. "Yeah. It was Pauline... and... and... Tabby. Tabitha."

At the mention of Tabitha's name, Brubaker felt his blood ice over. He had promised her he'd find her child. It was a promise he hadn't been able to uphold. The trauma of a missing child was too much to bear, how would she feel upon discovering her friend had been mutilated beyond recognition? Brubaker decided to put off confronting Tabitha. He'd speak to Pauline first.

"Sir," one of the paramedics came up and tapped Brubaker's shoulder. "If you want to talk to him, He'll be at Amherst Medical—"

"No." Brubaker stepped away from the ambulance. "I mean... I'll catch up with ya'all later. You're good to go."

A few minutes later, Giorgio was being carried away from the bar's parking lot. Brubaker was left behind. His hands sat in his pockets and his teeth gnawed on his tongue. Behind him, a camera flashed. They were taking another round of pictures of the blood splatters.

That had been last night. Now, it was morning, and Brubaker was at Pauline's house. It was a bit of a mess, but Brubaker couldn't judge. He lived alone in a studio apartment, ever since Francine had left him. He ate microwaved dinners and watched reality TV in his spare time. Pauline was raising six little ones as a full-time mom. She got a pass for skipping a few dishes and letting the laundry pile up.

The sink was overcrowded, the yard was littered with toys, and down the hall two siblings were fighting over the bathroom. Pauline kept her voice at a whisper, cradling a toddler to her side. She covered one of his ears, as if he could comprehend what the grown-ups were talking about.

Brubaker was joined by his partner. A young and raven-haired woman named Jill Roundhouse. Jill was a novice, so she remained unobtrusive while Brubaker explained –in compassionate words—to Pauline that her best friend had been turned into roadkill. Brubaker glanced at Jill from the corner of his eye, knowing that she was even more rattled by the corpse than he was.

"Dead?" Pauline asked for the fourth time, holding back tears.

"Yes ma'am. I'm sorry to be the one to tell you this... but we need to know whatever you know."

Pauline shook her head. "Oh, god. She was so young. And she had two children. Is Giorgio okay?"

"He's about as okay as any husband would be in his situation." Brubaker pulled a toothpick out and stuck it in his mouth. He'd been chewing on toothpicks since he quit smoking five years ago. After the last few hours, he was considering a relapse.

"I just can't believe it." Pauline frowned. "I mean, was it a random... killer?"

"We don't know. This is why any information you have could be vital to us." Jill stated in an impatient tone.

Brubaker held out a hand, signaling for calm. Jill's face matched her red lips.

"Pauline, we know it's a lot to take in. But please, just tell us... was there anything weird that happened at the bar? Did any guys try and pick Esther up or... or was there anyone with a bad vibe."

"No." Pauline shook her head. "No, there were a few people there, but they didn't really pay us much mind." Pauline paused, digesting her thoughts. "There was... there was the phone call. But that was for Tabby, not Esther."

"Phone call?"

"Yeah. Tabby didn't tell us much about it, but she got a weird phone call. It was obscene, I think." Pauline's face went white. "And it wasn't on her cellphone either. Someone called the bar and asked for her. Oh, God. Do you think that was... the murderer?"

"Did Tabby tell you anything about the caller?" Jill asked.

"I can't remember." Pauline clutched her toddler close. He was squirming in her arms. "I drank a lot. I mean, not too much. I was still good to drive, sir. But, uh, you know." She trailed off and turned her face toward the window. "You'd have to talk to her about it. God."

"Is there anything else you can remember? Anything at all?" Brubaker asked.

Pauline pursed her lips. "You just... you just never know what people are capable of."

Brubaker was becoming all too familiar with what people did to one another. And he didn't like it one bit.

Chapter Eleven
Voyeur

Irwin licked his cracked lips.

He rubbed his dick without any lotion.

His shaft was riddled with pimples and blisters.

His fingers were calloused and unyielding.

But he was too excited not to touch himself.

On the middle screen, a recording was playing. Daddy had gotten Tabby to tell her husband to kill himself. The tremble in her voice and the disbelief in his made it so *fucking* sexy.

Irwin had wanted to save his spunk for the real challenges ahead of her, but he couldn't help it. He was too turned on to *not* jerk himself off.

His eyes wandered toward the screen to his left. On it was a recording from a previous game. A woman was fitting a plastic funnel up her exposed ass, and Daddy's masked helper was aiming his cock toward it. Irwin had seen the video before. Markos had pissed into the funnel and filled the woman's ass up with his waste. They had then made her squat over a glass jar and drink the runny confection that spilled out of her rectum.

That had been a good one.

They had been holding her senile grandma hostage. The woman had done everything up until the very last task. When Daddy presented it to her, she had refused. Grandma had been killed. Her face had been peeled off on camera and it was shoved into her rubbery snatch. She had screamed herself hoarse.

The last task was always the same... no matter what. Everything beforehand was up to Daddy. He took suggestions, but when inspiration struck he ran with it. But the last task... was always the same.

Irwin wondered what Tabby would do.

Would she be capable of following through with it?

For some contestants. It was easy. For others... it was harder than any of the torment they had undergone before.

Some of the people on Daddy's livestream liked to pretend they weren't jerking off to the game. They said they were interested in the psychology behind it. They insisted they were only morbidly curious to see what people did when confronted with two abhorrent choices. Let someone die, or debase yourself?

Irwin held no such proclivities. He just liked to watch women suffer. He liked it when Daddy targeted men and children too, but not as much as women.

Irwin had never had a girlfriend before.

He thought himself a nice guy... but he didn't think women liked "nice guys". They saw his fat belly and acne-scabbed face and turned away from him. They didn't know what they were missing.

He pulled on his tiny penis and moaned as a dot of pre-ejaculate bloomed out of its crusted tip. His dick cheese was being converted into a yellowed paste. Irwin leaned forward, his belly almost swallowing up his cock.

He didn't use a tissue... he just watched as his dick spat a snotty rope of cum between his thighs. It splatted against the carpet beneath his computer desk. It would be left to turn into a crackly glaze there.

Without even wiping, he shuffled his shorts back up his hips and leaned back. Satisfied and happy. His underwear was already turning damp. He hadn't changed his briefs in about a week. A sticky streak of cum and urine had started to morph into a fungus in his drawers. His pubes itched and his skin was breaking out into a red rash, but Irwin didn't care. Sometimes, he liked to scratch his sores open and sniff his fingers afterwards. On other days, he'd milk them and use their rotten cream as lube.

Irwin sighed and looked toward the wall where a picture of an anime girl was hung. She was dressed as a maid and her skirt was so short it exposed the cleft in her panties. Her mouth was a tiny little O. About the size of a dime.

Irwin wondered once more why he didn't have a girlfriend. He was a gentleman if anything. Sure, he liked to watch horrible things happen... and he had suggested some ideas for the evening's events... but it wasn't like *he* was actually the one pushing Tabby to do those dreadful things.

He turned his eyes toward the third screen. On it, a livestream was running from the inside of Daddy's van. Daddy and Markos were both masked, but the little girl was not. Her burned eyes seemed to plead sightlessly for help. She had a gag secured over her mouth so she couldn't speak.

Daddy was on a speakerphone, talking to Tabby.

"Go to the barn. The first task is waiting for you there."

Irwin squirmed in his seat. He didn't think it was possible, but his cock was already stiffening once more.

"This will save little Riley's left arm... if you complete it. If not, we'll cut it away from her body. And we'll take videos too, Tabby. We'll take videos and share them to your Facebook friends."

Irwin licked his lips again. His tongue felt a

blister burst open and fill his mouth with salty droppings. He ignored the tart texture and leaned toward the screen.

He knew Daddy and Marko had collected the cowboy's body yesterday. He wondered if that would have anything to do with the first task.

As much as Irwin hoped to see his suggestions come to life, he trusted Daddy. When Daddy got an idea... it was usually grand.

Chapter Twelve
Unlucky Cowboy

At Daddy's behest, Tabby left her house and stumbled toward the barn. She looked up at the sky as she walked, expecting to see a drone bearing down on her from the heavens. But the sky was baby-blue and clear. There weren't even any clouds in sight. It was as if the world had been emptied while she was asleep, and now she was stuck with Daddy and his fiendish accomplice. She could only hope to appease them. Anything for the sake of her daughter.

Tabby felt sweat crawl down the small of her back. She was nervous. She had no clue what was in store for her, but it would certainly be depraved. Having completed only one task for Daddy was trying enough as it was.

Tabby opened the door to her barn and stepped in. The air inside was fetid and musty. The floor was caked in bird shit and feathers. She had been meaning to clean the place up, but the barn really served no purpose to her or Randy. It had come with the property. Aside from giving her goats a place to wander, it really offered them nothing. There were some stockades where horses had once been kept and a few rusty pieces of farm equipment... but that was it.

Tabby realized that she wasn't alone in the barn.

She gasped with fright when she saw that Daddy's heavy was with her. Muscled, dressed in a tank top and a grey pair of sweatpants, and wearing a featureless mask, he looked like the villain from a cheap 80's slasher movie. The type of flick Randy would watch for fun before the world treated him to a dose of real horror.

"Do you see my associate?" Daddy asked into Tabby's ear.

"Y-yes." She quivered.

"His name is Markos."

Shit. Why is he giving me his name? Maybe it's an alias. Or... maybe they don't expect you to talk to the police about this. Or maybe... oh god... maybe they're going to kill you.

She couldn't waste time thinking about that possibility. It was becoming more and more real with each passing second, but she figured she could repress it until it was a necessary woe.

"Say 'hi' to him."

"Hi, Markos."

The masked man waved a calloused hand. His shirt was smeared with dried blood. Esther's. Tabby didn't even have to ask. This was the man that had torn her head away from her shoulders... and set it on Riley's lap.

Tabby shuddered with revulsion and anger.

"What's the first task?" Tabby asked.

"I'm glad you're so high-spirited. Most folks aren't so eager to play."

"Please. Let's just get this over with."

"You'll follow Markos."

Markos took out a cell-phone. He tapped the screen slowly, and then held it in front of him. The light beaming out from its top indicated that he was filming.

"Markos will also be your cameraman. Just act like he isn't there when you get started."

Tabby saw that Markos had an erection. The swollen lump in his pants was becoming an arrow-head. His free hand reached down and pressed against his sturdy genitalia.

Is he going to rape me? Tabby thought with dread.

Markos began to walk backwards. He continued to film Tabby, seemingly interested in her response as he led her toward the back of the barn. He indicated one of the horse-stalls with a nod.

"You'll find your first task in there, Tabby." Daddy said into her cell-phone.

Tabby allowed Marko's to pull the gate open and expose the interior of the stall.

It was painted red.

Lying on his back, the cowboy from the bar was

almost unrecognizable. He had been stabbed so savagely, he looked like a victim of a big-cat attack. Slashes ran through his throat, tearing open his windpipe and exposing the white of his esophagus. His belly was so filled with punctures, it looked like compost. Even his pubic region had been mutilated with knife-wounds.

His pants had been dragged down to his ankles and his penis was exposed. It lay flat against his pubic mound. His ball sack had been cut open and his testicles hung out—attached to thin wires.

Tabby dropped the phone as she spewed vomit out of her trembling mouth. A hot blast of stomach bile and acidic oils sprayed out between her teeth and sizzled against the hay and scat caked floor. Tabby clutched her chest as another wave of nausea punched her.

"Radical." Markos spoke for the first time since Tabby had met him. He craned his neck around so that he could watch her hurl as he filmed her.

Tabby wiped her mouth with the back of her hand and scooped the phone up before the puddle of puke crawled over it. She held the phone to her ear and shuddered.

"You didn't have to kill him..."

"Yes." Daddy said. "I did."

"Why?"

"Because he's part of the game now. He's

you're first task, Tabs."

Tabby shook her head. A strand of mucus hung out of her nose and seeped into her sealed lips.

"Y-you... you're..."

"I'm evil." Daddy said calmly. "You're talking to an evil man. I don't feel guilty or remorseful when I do these things. I feel... electric. I feel accomplished and proud. That's who you're talking to. And it will go better for you if you don't act surprised at every corner of this voyage."

Tabby shut her mouth and released a bitter sob. He was right. She knew what he was and stating the obvious wasn't going to bring Riley back into her arms. She just had to swallow whatever pill he gave her. Tabby just had to persist.

"What do you want me to do?" Tabby asked.

"Look at that corpse."

Tabby did as she was instructed.

"I want you to fuck it."

Daddy might as well have dropped a load of bricks on Tabby's chest. Her heart stopped mid-beat and more bile began to scrabble its way up her throat. Like fire rushing up from a volcano.

She tried to replace fear with logic. How was she supposed to have... sex... with a corpse? It wasn't like the cowboy could get an erection. Was she expected to hump his limp cock and fake an orgasm? What was expected of her? The possibilities felt both endless and scant all at once.

"How?" She asked.

"I was hoping you'd ask that. Set the phone down and do what Markos says. It's okay. He's recording everything. You don't need to talk to me. I won't hold your hand through this."

Tabby began to look around for a place to put the phone.

"Oh, and Tabs?"

"What?"

"If you fail... I'll cut off Riley's left arm and I'll make her eat it to the bone." His tone was so dry it may as well have been a pound of flour.

Tabby closed her eyes. She imagined putting a gun in Daddy's mouth and pulling the trigger. She opened her eyes and found herself staring at the cowboy's carcass. She didn't even know his name.

And she was expected to have sex with his remains.

"Markos will guide you. I'll call you when it's over." *Click.* The phone went dead in her hand. She pulled it away from her face and looked at the blank screen with repugnance.

Markos stepped up to Tabby. He was uncomfortably close. The egregious bone in his pants was leaping toward her, as if it was a ferret trying to wriggle away from an affectionate owner. Tabby kept her head up and looked through the eye-holes of Markos's mask. His eyes were dewy and dumb. Like a teenaged boy.

Markos held his camera-phone up to her face. "Get undressed." He commanded.

Tabby didn't say anything. She had frozen over.

"Now!" He barked.

Tabby jumped. Tenderly, she reached up and pulled her tee-shirt over her head. She hadn't been wearing a bra. Her chest and face flushed red as Markos angled the camera down and captured a shot of her breasts. Without asking for her consent, he used his free hand to paw at her. His calloused thumb flicked her right nipple, urging it to stand. It was disobedient. So, he pinched it and made Tabby shriek with fright. His nails were like yellowed talons. He could have severed her nipple from her breast with one squeeze if he wanted to.

"The pants." He ordered.

Tabby tossed her shirt aside, wishing she could cover up again. Her heart was beating so loud it reminded her of a church bell.

She undid her buttons and shuffled out of her jeans. They thumped against the mossy floor, and she stepped away from them slowly. Markos hunched down, pointing the camera directly at her clothed crotch. His hand grabbed at her, pushing her genitals beneath her panties. His thumb moved the underwear aside, exposing her slit.

They're looking at me. They're looking at me on their phones and on their computers... and this is exciting for them. Oh, God. They all deserve to die.

Tears were raining down her cheeks, but she held her sobs back. She didn't want to appear weak to her audience of perverts.

"Take 'em off." Markos growled.

She did as she was instructed.

Fully nude, she looked cautiously toward the cowboy. She realized that she could smell feces coming up from his bloated corpse. The thought of touching him almost made her vomit all over again.

"Turn him over." Markos said and stepped away from her, framing the shot so that it captured the body in all its putrid glory.

Tabby covered her mouth with one hand and stepped into the stall. She moved slowly, as if delaying the act would somehow make it all stop. But there was no stopping whatever this was. She realized, as she hunkered down beside the corpse, that she should follow Daddy's advice. Just do things quickly and it would all be over.

With a grunt, she heaved the body over. Flopping onto his face, the cowboy's rear was exposed. Hay and chunks of gravel were welded onto his blood and scat spattered buttocks. Something was wrong with his anus, she noted.

There was a protrusion sticking out from it. Oily black and made of rubber.

"Pull it out." Markos said.

Tabby couldn't believe what she was seeing. Her tears dried as fear was replaced with genuine shock.

"Pull it out of him."

Tabby reached out and touched the rubber tool. It felt slimy.

"Do it!" Markos roared.

Tabby didn't hesitate. She grabbed the dildo and pulled. It came out with a belching pop. Anal fluids squirted out with its exit.

The dead man's sphincter burped before releasing a load of feces. The dildo had acted as a dam, but now that it was gone there was nothing containing the cowboy's projectile shits. They sprayed his inner thighs and quilted the ground. Musty and the color of iced tea. His body porridge made Tabby heave, but she had nothing left in her stomach to expunge.

She held up the dildo and looked at it with wide eyes. It was greased in fecal matter and gore. It was as long as her forearm, putting to shame every object she had ever inserted into her body previously. It was pitch black and its head was shaped like a massive almond.

"Turn him back over." Markos's voice was calm now.

Tabby did as she was commanded. Turned

over, his cock had been covered in his liquid diarrhea. It now looked like a stick of melted chocolate.

"Put the dildo on him." Markos said.

Tabby didn't know what to do. The dildo didn't come with a strap or a suction pad. She tried to balance it against the cowboy's pubic mound. She had to keep her hand on its veiny shaft just to keep it upright.

"Now... ride."

Just do it. Just do it and it will be over.

Tabby stepped over the body and spread her legs open. She tried not to think about the human materials that lubed the shaft of the sex-toy, or of the excrement pool in front of her. With her rear facing the cowboy's face, she lowered herself into a squat above the dildo.

Tabby froze, the head of the false cock a mere centimeter away from her dry vaginal hole. She took a deep breath and tried to pray. But if there was a God, he felt so distant it didn't even seem worth trying.

She groaned as she pushed the dildo into her. A bead of sweat grew over her brow, and she pinched her eyes closed. The pain was both physical and mental. It drew its claws through her heart and tore up her spirit.

She ground her teeth into her tongue... and began to ride.

For the Sake Of

Chapter Thirteen
The Short Way Home

Randy's parents were out. He had been alone when he'd received Tabby's terrible phone call. Her request rang through his head like a dinner bell.

Randy held his trusty compactable knife and weighed it in his hand. Its fine toned edges held so many potentials.

Randy sealed his eyes and imagined pressing the blade into the crook of his elbow and drawing it down. He imagined unzipping his arms and watching the blood steam out of him. A soupy stew of fluids and dancing cords.

It'd make her happy, knowing I cried while I died.

Randy had never contemplated suicide before. Even after Riley's disappearance. He just never had it in him. But now that Tabby had said the word, it had knit itself into his brain and refused to budge.

"Kill yourself." He muttered and looked at his reflection in the mirror.

And why shouldn't he? It had been eight months since *he* had lost their daughter. It had

been about that long since he had last heard
Tabby say she loved him with any meaning.
Even his parents took so much pity on him, he
barely felt like a real human being. Just a
Dickensian orphan in men's sized clothing.

Randy wondered how he'd do it. Tabby hadn't
provided instructions. What would make her
happy? A bullet through his skull? A cut along
his wrists? Maybe she wanted him to take a pill-
cocktail or step in front of a passing train.

She hadn't sounded angry. She sounded
resolved. As if she had been goaded into saying
what she said. As if saying it was a relief to her.

How long had she been wishing him dead?
Had she been harboring these feelings since
Riley's disappearance? Randy couldn't know. All
he had were speculations.

Randy rubbed his bearded chin and sighed
heavily. He wasn't going to kill himself. It wasn't
in him. But he was going to get out of Tabby's
life. It was clear she had no use for him anymore,
and the last thing he wanted to be was an
obstacle impeding her happiness and closure.

Something is wrong.

The thought hit him like a bolt of lightning.

*You didn't expect her to say that because it's
not like her. Randy, you know her. You know if
she wanted you gone, she'd simply have told
you she wanted a divorce. She's a blunt person
but she's not a psycho. And even if she did mean*

*what she said, that only means she needs help.
That may have been her shouting for help and
you're going to just drop away like an
uncommitted spectator? You're her husband
GODDAMNIT.*

Randy shook his head. She would have told
him. She would have called and let him know
she needed help. Tabby wasn't the type to skirt
around the issue. She was direct. She was cold—

—but the voice in his head was right. This was
so unlike her... it was really as if she had been
replaced with another person entirely.

Randy sighed. He snapped his knife closed and
affixed it to his belt. He walked out of the
bathroom and into his childhood bedroom. His
parents had immortalized his teenaged years
there. Hanging above his bed was a poster for
the film *Predator 2*. His desk was covered in old
comic books and magazines. He used to keep
some nudies under his bed, but his mother had
discreetly tossed them—along with a few crusty
gym socks—out while he was in college.

He felt too big for his old room. Unpacking his
drawers and loading them into his suitcase was
like watching a bull step around eggshells. After
packing, he thumped down the stairs. He wrote a
quick note explaining to his parents that he had
had to go home unexpectedly. He claimed it was
an emergency at work. They wouldn't question
that. If all went smoothly, no one but Tabby and

Randy would have to know about this awful phone call which was summoning him away from their safety and comfort. He loved his parents, but he was sure they would try and interject themselves into the situation. Tabby didn't need that.

Not that Randy knew exactly what Tabby needed, but he knew he wouldn't find out if he sat on his ass and did nothing. He was going to go home, and he was going to check on her.

He was going to ask her what she needed from him. If it was a divorce, he'd grant it. If she truly meant those horrible words, he didn't want to be married to her anyways.

But, if she was calling for help... he'd be there.

He hadn't been there enough.

Chapter Fourteen
Fuck It

Tabby screamed. Not with pleasure. Pleasure was impossible in a situation like this. She screamed out of anger and spite. She screamed out of fear and misery. She screamed at God and wished he would die. She screamed at herself, wishing she could have saved Riley before all of... this had become necessary. She screamed at Daddy and Markos. Again, she imagined plugging them with bullets. She imagined tearing their insides out of their bellies and forcing them to eat their internal stew. She screamed and wished she had never been born.

And mostly, she screamed because she was fucking a corpse.

The body trundled beneath her, moving with her thrusts. Its juices squirted out of its battered holes. It had been stabbed so much; riding it was like squeezing a sponge. She tried her best to avoid touching it, but she had to brace herself against something as she thumped her pelvis up and down the faux-dick.

She tried to think about anything other than the slimy substance greasing the dildo. She was certainly going to walk away with an infection, among other maladies. Who else had this toy penetrated before it was shoved up the cowboy's rectum?

The cock slipped backwards and out of her vagina. Its head thumped against the edge of the cowboy's opened wounds. She felt cold blood spackle her inner thighs.

Tabby reached between her legs and behind her, hoping to grip the dildo and put it back where it belonged. Instead, her fingers grazed one of his ruined pubic scars. Her fingers dipped in, becoming lost in the mushy hole where he had been stabbed.

A shiver of pure revulsion clenched Tabby's body.

She put the dildo back upright and lowered herself onto it, knowing it was doused in more corpse-juice didn't make it any grosser. She was already beyond the point of surprise.

Tabby opened her eyes and looked at her videographer. Markos was squatting down so he could capture the intrusion up close. While he was distracted, Tabby looked around the stall. She wondered if finding a weapon was even worth it. If she killed Markos, Daddy would just speed away with Riley in tow.

No. She was stuck in a corner she couldn't squirm out of. She just had to keep doing what they wanted, or else it was all over. Her poor little girl would have her arm chopped off... and she was certain Daddy would do as he had promised. Riley would be forced to chew as much of her arm flesh as she could until Daddy was content.

She couldn't comprehend how someone could enjoy doing these things to her and her baby. It was unfathomably evil.

How long had she been performing? She didn't know. Anywhere between five minutes and an hour. Her head was foggy with trauma and anger.

Markos stood, capturing her face. Snot was bubbling out of her nose and glazing her lips. Her mouth hung open and her face was red and puffy.

"Keep going." He insisted and reached down. Without even a shred of grace, he pulled his sweats down and exposed the most disgusting penis Tabby had ever seen. Markos was diseased. Warts and scabs grew out of his shaft and his cock-head was gummy with uncleaned sex-phlegm. She looked away but couldn't stop herself from listening to his strokes. It was like listening to two pieces of sandpaper rub together.

"Keep going." Markos said again.

Tabby looked up. His dick was a pole launching back and forth in his palm. Some of his scabs had burst and he was using his juices as lube.

She wondered how he was keeping the camera steady.

"Keep going!"

He didn't realize that this would become her mantra. As long as she kept going, she knew there was hope that she would be reunited with her little girl. There was nothing on earth Tabitha Moss wouldn't do for her daughter.

Tabby ground her teeth together and continued to ride. Markos rocked his head back and his cock spat out a dismal load. The stringy knot of sperm splattered against the floor between the cowboy's ankles. Maybe he had intended for it to hit her face, but his cock snot hadn't spurted the way it did in the pornos. Instead, it simply fell out of his dick in a few measly chunks.

Without even shaking, he stuffed his member back into his greasy sweats and took a deep breath. Markos stepped back and shut the camera off. "Okay, you can stop." He looked at his phone. "Wow. You rode that thing for forty-five minutes. You should be proud."

Tabby stood slowly. Gunk and black curds fell out of her vagina and trailed down her thighs. Her pelvis was so sore, it felt like she was about to pass a kidney stone.

"Can I get dressed?" She asked.

Markos didn't respond. Instead, he stepped back and indicated that she should leave the stall.

When she did, the cellphone Daddy had gifted her started ringing.

"Bravo!" Daddy proclaimed the moment the phone was answered. "Jesus Christ! You can ride a fuckin' dick!"

"Can I get dressed?" Tabby asked stoically.

"No. The viewers prefer you like this." Daddy snickered. "Oh, if only Riley could see you now."

Tabby ground her teeth into her tongue. It was becoming a scratched nub.

"Did you... did you take her... for this?" Tabby asked. She felt she was owed an explanation.

"I didn't abduct her." Daddy responded quickly. "No. I just bought her."

"You..."

"I got her *used*."

There was no more fight in Tabby at the moment. She had used it all to survive the first task. So instead of screaming at him, the way she was certain he had wanted her to, Tabby sighed and pinched her brow.

"You're evil." She said.

"I know." He returned. "Do you want a break?"

"No. No. Fuck it. Let's get on with it. Second task. Let's go."

"That's my girl."

Chapter Fifteen
Nails and Nails and Nails

Tabby walked back to her house nude. The sun beat down on her. Her whole body felt sticky, as if she had gotten caught in a glue trap and had only just wormed her way loose. Markos stood at the barn door and watched as she traveled back to her home. He didn't follow her, much to her relief. Whatever the second task was, it was hers to complete and hers alone.

Tabby walked into her home a different woman than the one she had been this morning.

"What do you want me to do?" She asked.

"This will be for Riley's right leg." Daddy intoned. "If you don't complete the second task, I'll remove it... and I'll have Markos bring it up to *you* to eat."

"Just tell me... what you want me to do." Tabby said wearily.

"I want to know what kind of mother you are." Daddy said dramatically. "You're obviously willing to do anything for Riley, but are you willing to lose something for her too?"

Tabby felt her guts churn. She wished she could shower. The dead man's noxious odors still clung to her. Her vagina was dripping curdled offal and her legs were so sore they may as well have been worked over by an inexperienced acupuncturist.

"I want you to pull your nails out." Daddy said.

"What?"

"Set up the phone and record yourself. No one wants to miss this."

"Wait." Tabby insisted. "How?"

"Get creative, Tabs. Go to the camera app and hit 'record'. I'll still be here. I'll be with you at every step of this amazing journey. Pull your nails out, Tabby... and I won't pull anything off of Riley."

That first task had drained her so much, Tabby wasn't certain she could withstand more pain. Much less the self-inflicted variety. But she had to. She had to.

Keep going.

"Fuck. I don't know what to use. I don't know what to—"

It struck her. Randy kept his tools in the basement.

Running down the stairs was a task unto itself. And a trying one. Her legs wobbled as she went. After flicking the light on, her eyes fell onto Randy's red tool chest. Her dad had gotten him that chest as a wedding present.

Don't think about it. Just keep going. You're almost there.

Tabby threw the chest open and dug around. She exhumed a pair of rusty pliers.

The video started and Daddy was greeted to an unattractive shot of Tabby sitting at her dining room table. She was naked and her flesh had gone grey. Hay stuck out of her matted hair, making her look like a fucked-up scarecrow. She was so sweaty she appeared to have just stepped out of a sauna.

Good. The nastier the better. Daddy thought as he put a cream soda to his lips and took a long sip. His captive child rustled about in the corner. Zip-tied and abused, she and her mother made a fitting pair.

Daddy laughed and watched the video.

Tabby showed her fingers off to the camera. She was really a natural. He couldn't have chosen a better victim.

"This is for Riley." She muttered. Her tongue was dry, and her eyes were soaked.

She took the pliers and began to clasp her left thumbnail with them. She took a deep breath and paused before she cracked the nail back. It happened so fast; Daddy couldn't believe she had actually done it. The nail shattered down the middle, like an icy pond with too much weight on it.

Tabby paused, and then unleashed an unholy scream. It outmatched the noises she had made while fucking the corpse.

Blood began to seep out of the injured nail. But that didn't stop Tabby. She wriggled the nail loose and pulled it away from her finger. Bloody strands connected the two. Uncovered, the bed of her finger was a nest of raw nerves and bleeding liquids.

Tabby set the nail down on the table and leaned back. Her eyes were pinched shut and Daddy could see she had bitten her bottom lip. Blood eased out from the wound and trickled down her chin.

"Okay. Okay." Tabby said aloud. "N-nine more to go."

She began to work the pliers around her index fingernail. It was almost too much for Daddy. He could feel his penis stiffening between his legs. He'd need a receptacle for his seed.

He leaned over and picked up Esther's decapitated head. He worked the mouth open and gingerly pulled his manhood out from his jeans.

He didn't take his eyes off the screen. He watched hungrily as Tabby pulled out her fingernails... one after the other.

Tabby was done. She set herself back into her chair and looked down at the nails scattered in front of her. A pool of blood grew beneath both hands. Her fingers were soaked in it. She had never experienced such pain before, but she had done it. All ten of her fingers were naked. *Nails grow back*, she reminded herself. *Daughters legs don't.* As terrible as this had been, she was eerily proud of herself. She had suffered in place of Riley for once. And that poor darling had suffered so much. If Tabby had to pull out all of her toe-nails too, she'd have done it.

"Very good." Daddy said from the cell-phone's speaker. "I'm so proud of you, Tabs."

"Fuck you." Tabby breathed.

"Do you need a break?"

"No. Third task. Let's go."

"No, Tabby... I think you're being dishonest. You've done more in the last two hours than even I expected. You're going to need your strength for what comes next."

"I don't want a break." Tabby declared. "I want to finish this. I want... I want it to be over."

She looked at her scarlet hands and began to weep. She had lost so many fluids, even her sobs were dry.

"Please, it's worse if we wait. It's torture. I just want to finish this and see my baby!"

Daddy paused and then unleashed a long sigh. "Do you want to talk to her? Would that help?"

Tabby felt her brain and heart turn to mush. She forgot that this was Daddy's fault and that they were enemies. She would do whatever he wanted just to speak to her child one more time.

to earn the privilege of hearing Riley's voice.

"Y-yes." Tabby confirmed with a whimper. "Please."

She heard a lot of shuffling and a dry command: "It's your mom. Remember what we said."

She could hear soft breathing.

Riley.

Tabby could have fainted.

"H-hi, angel." Tabby said. "I'm... I'm here."

"Mom?" The girl said. Her voice sounded weak and raspy, as if she hadn't had a drink of water in days. As if she was crawling through the dessert in search of an oasis, and all she had found were mirages. Tabby couldn't bear the distance between her and her child.

"Yes! It's me! Oh, God. Are you... are you okay, hon?"

"I'm... you sound different." The girl said.

"I know, honey. I know. I'll see you soon, okay? I'm going to get you away from them."

"Please."

The phone was whisked away and suddenly Daddy's voice filled it. "Is that better?"

"Yes." Tabby nodded.

"Are you going to give yourself a break before the third task?"

"Yes."

"Good. I'll call you."

Click.

Tabby didn't know how long her wait would be. She leaned forward and looked at her hands. She needed to do something about them. They were frayed and electric. The agony was overwhelming.

She stood and wandered toward the kitchen sink.

Turning on the faucet took some time and dousing her sore digits beneath the cold water was torturous. But she bit her lower lip and bore through it.

She needed to be *somewhat* refreshed before Daddy called her back. If she wore herself out, then the game was as good as lost.

She went to the hall bathroom and used a sanitary wipe to clean her vagina as best she could.

She didn't want to risk taking a shower in case she missed Daddy's call. So, she used wet wipes and a soaked towel to sponge away the corpse-grease that covered her naked body. As she worked, she thought of her mantra.

Keep going. Keep going. Keep going.

Soon, it would all be over.

Tabby didn't hear the knock at the door. But she did hear the phone ring. She scooped it up and held it to her ear.

"Did you call the fucking cops?" Daddy's voice was incised with panic.

"What?" Tabby's face went white. "What?"

"You stay in your fucking house! You don't move a goddamn muscle! If you do, Riley's fucking dead! She's dead!"

Click.

Tabby felt like weeping all over again.

Chapter Sixteen
Bonus Round

Brubaker and Jill drove up the gravel road toward Tabby's farm.

They were focused on finding Tabby and figuring out what had happened to her friend. Brubaker needed to know who had called her. He was certain that that would be their first clue toward finding the murderer.

At least, he hoped so.

He stepped out of the cruiser first. Jill was quick to follow. She was wearing reflective aviators. She thought she looked like a badass when she wore them. Brubaker didn't really care about being perceived as anything other than what he was.

A simple cop who cares about his job.

He swirled his toothpick from one corner of his mouth to the other and strode up the steps toward Tabby's door. He gave the door a curt knock and stepped back.

Jill marched up to Brubaker's side and said: "What time is it?"

"I don't know. Still early." He checked his watch. "About nine."

"Nine is early for you?"

"Maybe she's hungover." He knocked again. "I don't know. Usually, she's quick to the door." Brubaker lowered his voice. "Most mothers of missing children are. They expect us to have news." Brubaker sighed. "I wish we did."

Jill ran a hand through her red hair and looked over her shoulder. She released a small gasp. "Whoa. Did you see that?"

Brubaker turned and tried to follow her eye line, but her ridiculous glasses made it impossible.

"Someone was in the barn." Jill whispered.

"Oh, it's probably Tabby."

"No." Jill glowered. "No. It was a guy."

Brubaker's jaw hung loose. His toothpick drooped out like a deflated flower. "A... guy?"

Had Randy come back from his hiatus? No. Jill knew Randy. She would've recognized him. Brubaker knew what Jill meant when she said, "a guy". She meant that the person in the barn was a stranger.

"What'd he look like?" Brubaker drew his sidearm. Jill followed his lead.

"Big. Dressed in a tank top and... wearing a mask."

"What type of mask?"

"All white. No features that I saw. He was watching us. The moment he realized I saw him he backed away. Not quickly either. Slowly. He knew he'd been caught but... he didn't run."

This is him. Brubaker thought with dread. *Who else could it be? A weird stranger in a mask hiding in a barn? God. It's like something out of a movie.*

"I'm going to go down and see what's going on, Jill. You call for backup."

"Right." Jill nodded and rushed away from the porch and toward the car. As she went, Brubaker started to amble toward the barn. He shouted out in an angry tone:

"This is the police! Come out with your hands up!"

No response. He hadn't really expected one.

"I will open fire if you do not comply!" Brubaker roared.

He stepped toward the barn and swung the door open. He swiveled on his hips, pointing the snout of his gun from one corner of the barn to the other. The smell hit him suddenly. The stench of rotten meat and an abandoned porta-potty. He felt a shiver of seasickness race through him.

"Come out with your hands up... *now!*" Brubaker proclaimed.

He heard a snicker from the nearest stall.

"Here piggy, piggy, piggy..." The man sang in a childish tone. His voice sent shivers down Brubaker's spine. He had met his fair share of crazies and maniacs before. Even in a quiet town like Amherst, where nothing ever happened. Usually, they were just drugged out looneys, or abusers. They were easy to wrangle, even when they smelled.

But this guy made all of those bastards smell like roses.

"Come an' get me!" The voice chirped.

Brubaker had interviewed a genuine psychopath once. The guy had been planning a school shooting and would have carried it out if his own bedraggled mother hadn't called the police. She'd found his diary and had read it and had been shocked by the meticulous plan he'd laid out.

While Brubaker spoke to the boy, he kept chittering, laughing, and smiling. As if it was all a big joke. As if it was a game.

This man in the barn was laughing the exact same way.

Brubaker turned around and was ready to squeeze the trigger... but his assailant was faster.

The masked man was holding a handgun.

He pulled the trigger so fast; Brubaker didn't even see the fiend's finger move.

Jill was halfway toward the cruiser when the gun went off. She spun on her heels and peered toward the barn. Her heart hammered in her ribs and her gun shook in her hand. Had

Brubaker gotten the bastard or was her partner and mentor in trouble? She was torn between running to the car and running to his aide. But it didn't matter.

By the time she had decided it was more practical to call for back-up, a weather van roared up the driveway. The vehicle growled as it leapt over bumps and mounds in the gravel.

The van parked between Jill and the cruiser.

She was confused but didn't realize she was in any danger until the van's door slid open and revealed a similarly masked man. Only this one was well-dressed. He was wearing a black duster, a pair of blood besmirched jeans, and a button up.

He was also carrying an Uzi.

The gun spat out a load of bullets which sprinkled across the gravel in front of Jill's feet. She shrieked and backpedaled, holding up her gun and squeezing off a round. The bullet dinged against the van's opened door and the masked assailant jumped back in shock.

He hefted up his assault rifle and squeezed the trigger, peppering Jill's legs with bullets. They tore through her knees and blasted her legs backwards, like a grasshopper's.

Jill slumped onto the ground, her bones jutting out from her destroyed limbs. Her eyes filled with tears and her sunglasses landed on the ground in front of her.

"*No!*" Jill roared. "*Noooo.*"

Her shooter stepped out of the van and strolled toward her leisurely. He stepped over her body and kicked the gun away from her fingers. She hadn't even considered firing at him while he approached. Her eyes were blinded by the pain beneath her thighs.

She looked up and saw, much to her horror, that he had a cell-phone strapped to his breast. It was recording a livestream of her assault.

"Whoa. Today just keeps getting better and better." The attacker prodded the back of her head with the still hot muzzle of his illegal firearm.

"You... I'm... I'm hurt... call... call..." Jill stammered.

She caught sight of something terrible within the chambers of the van. A diapered child was zip-tied to the leg of a desk which had been bolted down in the van's middle. The child's eyes were scabbed over and blind. She seemed unfazed by the gunfire. Next to her was a decapitated head, its mouth oozing with semen and blood.

Jill gazed up at the fiend overhead. "Oh, god." She muttered.

The butt of the Uzi collided with Jill's crown. She was knocked cold.

Brubaker slammed against the door to one of

the horse-stalls. His body was rippled with pain. The bullet had sunk its teeth into his right shoulder. Blood sputtered out like water from a blocked hose. The masked man watched as Brubaker struggled through the pain, his eyes delighted behind his featureless visage.

Brubaker tried to lift his gun, but his ruptured shoulder made the motion impossible. His eyes strained shut and tears oozed out from their corners. "Oh, God! You shot me!"

"Yeah, that was kind of the point." Markos chided and fired again. This time, he purposefully aimed for the air. A vortex of feathers and stray bits of hay fell down from the rafters above him.

Brubaker froze. The gun dropped out of his hand and landed with an ineffective thud on the ground. His right arm hung limply from its busted shoulder. His left was squeezing down on the wound. His skin was painted crimson. His lips trembled and his eyes scurried about like squirrels through dried leaves.

Markos pointed his spare index finger toward Brubaker and chuckled. "You've pissed your pants." He sounded like a school bully, taunting a weaker child. But Brubaker's face went tomato red and he squeezed his moistened thighs together.

"Who are you?" Brubaker asked. "What are you doing on Tabitha Moss's property?"

"We're just playing a little game." The man pulled his cell-phone out and held it up to his eyes. He was recording a video, Brubaker knew. He ducked his head down and looked away from the camera. Whatever this video was going to be, he wanted no part of it.

"Are you here because of the bitch from the bar?"

Brubaker's mouth went dry. "Y-yes."

"I killed her." Markos admitted, on video no less. "And I cut off her head. And my friend and I have taken turns fucking her mouth. You know what happens when you cum in a decapitated head? It drains out of her throat-hole. It doesn't run out either. It ebbs... like glue."

Brubaker looked up with red eyes. "Why?"

"I've killed a lot of people, officer. I've made them hurt too, before they died. You wanna hear about it?"

"No. I... no. Please, just let me go." His eyes darted toward his gun. He could reach it with his good hand... but if he tried he knew this monster wouldn't hesitate to shoot him between the eyes. And whoever he was, he was a good shot too. Brubaker knew, without a shadow of a doubt, that this fiend had meant to clip his right shoulder. He knew that this villain had wanted to keep him still but didn't want him incapacitated. Not totally. He also knew that pleading was worthless. But he did it anyways. "I won't tell anyone. I'll just get in my car and leave."

Markos snickered. "You want to leave?"

"Yes."

"You won't tell a soul?"

"Yes."

"Bullshit." Markos grunted. "I don't believe you really want to leave. I don't think you even want to *live*."

"I do! More than anything." Brubaker looked toward the camera phone, as if he was counting on it to be more benevolent than its owner.

"Prove it." Markos snarled.

Brubaker wiped his sweaty brow with a scarlet fist. He whimpered and shook his head. "I don't know what you want me to say—"

"Look into the camera and tell me this. Say: 'I'm a useless pig and I want to save my bacon'." Markos released a keening laugh, as if his immodest pun was comedic gold.

Brubaker looked into the lens and did as he was asked. "I'm a useless pig and I want to save... my bacon."

"Now snort." Markos stepped closer. The gun's black hole seemed to grow into a hungry mouth to Brubaker's pain-fizzled eyes.

"Snort?"

"Like a piggy."

Brubaker released a small snuffling sound.

The gun fired. The bullet zoomed over his head and sent woodchips flying in every direction.

Brubaker lurched down—cowering and crying. He began to snort with bravado, imitating the pigs he had grown up with on his father's farm. He even attempted a few high-pitched squeals.

Markos laughed heartily, enjoying the show.

"Good! That's good! That's enough, dude! God." Markos snickered and lowered his gun but kept the camera up. "One more thing... and then I'll let you go."

"You promise?" Brubaker was out of breath. His shoulder was smarting something awful.

"I promise. Swear to God. Cross my heart." Markos said.

"I just want to go home—"

"You will. As long as you prove that you think it's worth it." Markos stepped forward. "As long as you do what I tell you to."

"Anything."

Markos smiled. "You have exactly 15 seconds to dig out one of your eyes and eat it. Starting now."

Brubaker felt his balls crawl into his belly. His spine began to tingle as the magnanimous horror of the man's request took hold.

"What?" Brubaker asked.

"One."

"Wait. This... this is insane."

"Two."

"Would you hold on and just tell me what you really want here?"

"Three."

"I've got money for cripes sake!"

"Four."

"Oh... oh... God. You mean it?"

"You're wasting time. Five. Six. Seven."

Brubaker felt his jowls tremble. He glanced around, looking for something he could use to pry his own eyeball out of its socket. The request was too demented to truly comprehend.

"Eight. Nine."

Brubaker reached up with his good hand and held it over his left eye. He closed his right and sucked in a deep breath.

"Ten."

He dug his thumb into the base of his eyeball. The lid flicked closed, and tears squirted out in response to the sudden intrusion. Brubaker screamed as his blood began to boil.

He didn't know if he could do it.

He began to work his finger into the socket, prying his eyeball free. His middle finger gripped the orb and the two digits worked in tandem to loosen it. Blood and orbital juices seeped between his fingers and slickened his palm. His whole body felt sticky and oily.

"Twelve." The man's voice was muffled. He was buried behind the pain that raced through Brubaker.

Brubaker pulled. His lids snapped shut over the extended length of red cord that still connected his eyeball to his head. He twisted the cord up like a pesky bit of twine and pulled with a sharp grunt. It snapped like a guitar string and fell back into its vacuous socket.

Now, the eyeball rolled around in Brubaker's palm like a marble. His other eye had gone fuzzy since it now carried the brunt of his vision and his agony.

"I did it... oh, Jesus."

You have to eat it too.

Brubaker felt his gag reflex tremble. But he knew it meant life or death. He put the orb up to his mouth and pushed it in. He sealed it beneath his slimy palm and struggled to swallow. He could feel the ball of juices push its way down his throat. It was like swallowing a wet tea bag.

Brubaker held his hand out and opened his mouth. He lifted his tongue so that his abuser could see he hadn't hidden his eye.

"See? See?" Brubaker said. "I... did... it."

"Yes you did. But... you took too long."

"What?"

"That was way longer than fifteen seconds. Sorry, buddy."

Brubaker waited for Markos to say that he was just kidding. That it was just a cruel joke. But instead, Markos raised his gun... and fired.

Part Three
Offal

Chapter Seventeen
Pig

The masked men had dragged the wounded cop into the house. Now, there was no barrier between Tabby and Daddy. He was younger than she had expected, and if not for the mask and the blood she could only assume he was a handsome man. His black hair was slicked back, and his fingers were trimmed and neat. He wore a long coat and a pair of tight-fitting jeans.

The hulking maniac by his side—Markos— slapped a raw tube of meat against the table. It was a penis, Tabby saw. She wasn't shocked by it. A dismembered cock was the least of her worries.

"I filmed a little bonus round with this little piggy." Markos sneered and plucked at the cock's purple head. "I took him apart afterwards for some gore-porn."

"Good job, man." Daddy said, as if Markos was an excellent employee and not a disturbed psychopath.

Both men turned and looked at Tabby as if she was roadkill.

"You called the goddamn cops." Daddy pointed

his gun toward Tabby.

"No! No! I didn't! I swear! I didn't!" Tabby pleaded. She clutched her hands together and dipped her head low.

On her kitchen floor, Jill was losing a massive amount of blood. It streamed out like water from a ruptured hose. With a few twists and turns, Tabby was sure those obliterated legs could be pulled completely from Jill's body. Tabby tried not to look at Jill and instead focused on the angry eyes behind Daddy's mask.

"You didn't call them? Huh?" Daddy asked. "Then why are they *here*?"

"Did she lose?" Markos asked. "Is the game over?"

Tabby glanced at the livestream on Daddy's chest and saw that the audience was vying for attention. She saw someone called *ARMANDRUMBLE69* say in all caps: "NO IT'S JUST GETTING GOOD!"

The disgust Tabby felt was overwhelming, but she needed to finish the game. If she didn't, Riley was dead. And Tabby knew she'd only blame herself until she wound up in an early grave.

She got down on her knees beside the quivering husk of injured cop-flesh and pushed her nail-less hands together. They became a red and ragged knot.

"Please, Daddy. Please. Maybe... maybe Randy

sent them for a wellness check, after I called him. Maybe... maybe they're here to ask me if I saw what happened to Esther. Maybe they just wanted to talk about Sunday's potluck. I don't know! But I can *promise* you I didn't call them!"

Like an obedient dog, she genuflected at Daddy's feet. She kissed his blood scuffed shoes and wrung her hands together at his pelvis.

"Please! Please, believe me! Oh, God! Please, believe me! I'll do anything! I'll do anything! Please!"

Markos released a giggle. Daddy stifled his laugh with a hand over his mask. His shoulders jittered with glee.

"What if I don't believe you?" Daddy asked after composing himself.

"I'll do anything to prove it! Please!" Tabby cried.

"Okay." Daddy stepped back. "Markos. Get her something good."

Markos began to shuffle through the drawers in Tabby's kitchen. He hummed to himself as he went. He pulled out a steak knife and held it up in the air, as if he was testing its weight. Then he shrugged and dropped it into the sink before returning to his rummaging.

"This next task isn't for Riley." Daddy said. "It's for you. If you fail, we'll know you've called the cops. We'll know the game was disrupted because of you. And we won't want to play anymore. I'll shoot you in the head, and Riley will live. But she won't live well. I'll sell her, Tabs. I'll sell her to people who will do terrible things to her. And that will be your fault."

Tabby gulped.

"But, if you do this... we go right back where we were. I'll trust you, and the game will continue. You got it?"

"Yeah." Tabby nodded and forced a grin. "Anything."

"Good."

Markos dropped a meat tenderizer on the kitchen floor. He kicked it toward Tabby. She looked at the tool and then back up at Daddy with sorrowful eyes.

"Beat that pig's head in." Daddy said. "And I'll believe this wasn't you're doing."

Once more, Tabitha was finding herself in a position where she could not win. If she did as Daddy asked, she'd be a murderer. Although, did such an act count if it was under duress? She didn't know the legality of it all. But she knew one thing. A life was going to be taken. And it was on her shoulders. She could either murder the lady-cop... or do nothing and allow Riley to suffer a far less merciful fate.

Tabby shook Jill's shoulder, rousing her. She took the meat tenderizer and clutched it close to her naked chest.

Jill was groggy. The pain of her collision with

Daddy's gun was still fresh. Her teeth felt loose, and her eyes were swampy. Jill looked up toward Tabby and smiled.

"Hey." She said. "Hey, are you... are you taking me home?" She sounded drunk.

Tabby shook her head.

Jill's face fell when she caught sight of Daddy looming over the two women.

"Oh, Christ..." Jill murmured.

"I'm sorry." Tabby said and held the tenderizer aloft. Its bumpy sides gleamed in the sunlight streaming in through the kitchen window. "They haven't given me any other choice." Tabby explained.

She needed Jill to know she wasn't killing her for fun.

She needed Jill to know that this wasn't her idea.

"Get on with it." Markos insisted, recording everything with his phone.

"I have to do this." Tabby said. "Or they'll murder my daughter."

Jill wheezed. Her breath was wet. She looked from Daddy to Tabby to Markos. Her legs were useless, and she was leaking out. Tabby knew that Jill would be dead in a few moments if left unattended. There was no way to help her. This awful thing that Tabby was about to do was a relative mercy. Yet still, her hands trembled, and she didn't know if she had the strength to bring the tenderizer down.

Jill made eye contact with Tabby. Her lips trembled and a stream of blood began to ooze out of her mouth.

"Do it." Jill rasped.

Tabby swung the tenderizer down. It collided with Jill's brow. The skin split open and blood welled up, but the blow hadn't been strong enough. It had glanced against her, but it hadn't killed her. It just uncovered the inner workings of her forehead. Red muscles were wound together like a length of licorice.

Blood seeped up and filled the ridges of her exposed musculature.

Jill's eyes became wet with fresh tears. Her mouth trembled beneath her vacuum-sealed lips. She stared up at Tabby with a mix of emotions.

Fear.

Anger.

Depression.

Understanding.

It almost made beating her again even worse, knowing that Jill understood why Tabby had to do what she was doing.

"Do... it." Jill rasped.

Tabby did.

She raised the tool and brought it down again.

This time, she threw more of her weight into the blow.

The implement smashed into Jill's nose.

Its bridge cracked open, and a fume of blood soused her face.

"Again!" Daddy yowled.

Tabby raised the tenderizer and brought it down. Jill's cheek bone popped out of place, but it didn't break through the skin. Her legs began to jitter, and a stream of piss ran down her thighs. Jill's breath came out in hectic bursts. She was having a panic attack.

"Again!"

Tabby struck her in the lower jaw. Several of Jill's teeth came loose and fell into her throat.

"Again!"

Tabby hit her on the brow again. Her head began to fall inward. Tabby hit her repeatedly. One successive blow after another. No hesitating. She hammered her face in.

Once, twice, thrice... ten times.

Jill's nose folded in on itself. Her teeth began to break through her lips. One eye swelled shut and the other deflated in its socket. Blood sputtered out of her mouth and from the numerous holes breaking across her busted visage.

"Stah-puh." Jill slurred. "Pwease."

Tabby rained down with fury. The meat tenderizer was caked in blood. Its blows brought up chips of bone.

Jill's skin seemed to melt away from her face,

shredded by the grooves in the tool. Blood sprayed in multiple directions. It filled Tabby's mouth and tinted her vision red.

Tabby leaned back and dropped the tenderizer. It hit the floor with a clang. Tabby sucked in a few shivery breaths and then observed the chaos and carnage she had wrought.

Jill's body was still. Her face was demolished.

She was dead.

She was dead.

She was dead.

And Tabby had killed her.

Chapter Eighteen
Back to Our Regularly Scheduled Atrocity

Tabby stared down at the dead policewoman. She willed Jill to take another breath. She wished that this was all a joke and that she hadn't really done these awful things. But, if it was a joke, it was on Tabby and no one else.

Jill was dead.

The cowboy was dead.

Brubaker was dead and his penis was resting on her table.

Tabby's hands were iced over with brutal pain. Her missing nails itched, and her pelvis was so sore, she felt as if it was filled with rocks.

And she was still only halfway through Daddy's awful game.

Tabby looked up and saw the bustling screen pinned to Daddy's chest. His viewers were happy with the murder. She saw positive emoji's dancing up the chat wall. Smiling faces, bursts of flame, and thumbs pointed upward. The sick fucks were satisfied.

Tabby looked up toward Daddy. His mask revealed nothing.

"Are you ready for your next task?" Daddy

asked gravely.

She nodded eagerly. "Yes."

"You'll need to prove to me that you'll do more than just love your daughter after we give her back to you. You need to prove... that you'll care for her."

"I can. I will. Tell me... what's the next task?"

"A mother bird will chew up a chick's food and deposit it into their mouths. Did you know that?"

Tabby nodded slowly.

"Would you do the same for your hatchling?"

"Yes. I would. Just give me a chance."

"I want you to show me." Daddy reached up and held the bottom of his mask. "I want you to feed the corpse."

Tabby waited for further instructions. Daddy's passion for dramatics made this excursion even more tortuous than it would be otherwise. He was always forcing her to wait for the full scoop.

"I'm going to feed you, Tabby. Then, you're going to feed the policewoman. And she better swallow every bit of it... or we'll chop off Riley's right arm. And we'll fuck you with it."

Tabby shook her head. She still didn't understand.

And then, Marko's had his arms around her. He hefted her up to her feet and took a handful of her hair. He twisted it around so that her head was held securely in his hand. He forced her down so that she was squatting on her haunches.

Tabby's eyes darted back and forth as Markos's arm snaked around her. Her clasped her jaw and squeezed, forcing her mouth to pop open.

Daddy stepped up and pulled his mask away from his face.

His face was so young and so earnest. He really did look like any other person. Tabby wouldn't have even noticed him in a crowd were it not for his steely eyes and wicked smile.

"This is for you, *ARM&RUMBLE69*!" Markos announced toward Daddy's camera.

Daddy let his mask sit atop his head like a malformed baseball cap. He opened his mouth and dug two fingers down his throat. He had come well prepared as a full banquet of fast food worked its way up his throat and out his maw. Before Tabby could even react to what she was seeing, his vomit spattered across her bare face. Curdled chunks of half-digested food filled her mouth and began to wriggle against her tongue. The pieces were so soft and chunky; they reminded her of a pound of cream-cheese. It tasted tangy and sour, slickened with stomach enzymes and acids.

Tabby coughed and squirmed in Markos's arms. She wanted to throw up again. The taste of Daddy's puke was too heinous. Tabby began to spew up his regurgitation. It trickled down her chin and between her breasts.

"Messy, messy!" Daddy chided between burps. He patted his stomach, as if he was fulfilled. "Now... feed the stiff."

Markos released Tabby. She fell down on the floor and exploded with coughs. Her skin felt electric. Her face was wracked with humiliation, anger, and pain. She curled into a shivering, fetal ball. Daddy's taste remained in her mouth.

"You have to put it in her mouth." Markos said and prodded her rear with his foot.

"I'm... I'm sorry." She hadn't been prepared for any of this. Maybe if they had warned her that Daddy was going to use her as a barroom toilet, she would have been ready. Or maybe a reaction like this was inevitable.

She looked over at the ground beside her. The spilled puke had coagulated with Jill's blood. The white curds had turned crimson, sopping up the spilled gore. It looked like cherry pudding.

"You want to give up?" Markos sneered.

"Really? After everything that's happened your gonna let a little barf stand between you and your daughter's safety? I'm disappointed in you, Tabs." Daddy lowered his mask back in place. "You fucked a dead guy. You pulled out all your fingernails. You fuckin' killed a bitch. But you draw the line at holding a little yuck in your mouth?"

"No." Tabby moaned.

"Why don't I just get Riley and put a fucking bullet in her brain, huh? Or better yet, why don't we dissect her right in front of you? Did you ever wonder what color her lungs are? I could fucking show you!" Daddy knelt down and smacked Tabby across the cheek. Her flesh immediately went red and began to swell. He smacked her again, hitting her with his opened palm. He took her head and pushed it against the wet floor, forcing her to swim in the sick confection that covered her kitchen. Tabby released an agitated groan. She reached up and pushed against his wrist.

"No. You don't fucking get to resist me. I own you. I own you until this is over." Daddy snarled and grabbed her by the hair. He lifted her head, exposing her to the camera. "You're my toy." He slapped her across the face with his opposite hand. It stung. Tabby felt herself go warm beneath her waist. She had pissed herself, much to her anguish. Urine hissed out, dredging up more chunks of the cowboy's body gravy, which had been buried deep in her vaginal tunnel.

"You fucking bitch." Daddy hit her again. "You're weak. You're weak. And Riley will suffer for it."

"Wait." Tabby whispered. "Wait."

Daddy slapped her again. Her cheek was raw now.

"Wait!" Tabby roared and held up a hand.

"Wait! Wait! Wait!"

Daddy held his hand up, preparing for another blow.

"I'll do it." Tabby said.

Daddy released her hair. He stood and stepped back so the camera could capture all the obscene action. Tabby looked over her shoulder. Markos was standing in the corner. Even he had been surprised by Daddy's abusive outburst.

Tabby turned and stared down at the bloody puddle of sick. She scooted toward it, holding her breath as if she was about to submerge herself into the deep end of a swimming pool.

She hovered over the puddle, her mouth inches away from it.

Then, like a dog, she began to lap it up.

Her tongue collected goblets of stinky food and stored it in her cheeks. She sealed her eyes shut and tried not to breathe in the tart and somewhat-fecal odors beneath her.

She lifted her head, holding the mouthful in. It was hard. Her gag reflex reacted naturally to the combination of blood and vomit in her mouth. She had to be quick.

She crawled over to Jill's corpse and worked her fractured jaws open. They parted with a wet pop. The blood had already started to turn sticky, and it was gluing her split lips together.

Tabby worked them loose and pried Jill's jaw open. Then, she poured the stew out from her mouth and into Jill's. It rained down on her wounded lips and seeped between her busted teeth. Her mouth was like a vortex of torn gums and tattered muscles. Tabby had to use her fingers to shove the vomit down her throat. But she managed it. Before long, it was draining from Jill's tongue down her hole.

"Good job." Daddy said in awe.

Tabby put her face against the ground and began to slurp up more of the belly-sauce. She could barely taste it now. The digestive fluid was muted by all the blood.

Mama Bird. I'm the Mama Bird. Tabby thought with an internal chuckle. *Look at me. I can feed my offspring, just like all the other Mamma Birds. Just like they do—*

She shuddered as she filled Jill's mouth with more jelly. She closed her eyes, not wanting to watch the dead girl as she swallowed up Daddy's refuse and her own blood.

"Such a good girl. See? I knew you had it in you. You just needed some encouragement." Daddy snickered.

Encouragement and abuse went hand-in-hand with Daddy, it seemed.

Tabby began to take in even more mouthfuls of the slime on her kitchen floor. She didn't want to think about it. She wished this chore was already complete and that they were moving onto the fourth and final task. She wished she could fast-forward to tomorrow.

I'll be in a hospital bed. And Riley will too. We'll be taken care of by people who care. We'll be better in no time.

Tabby hurled vomit into the rancid cave which had once been Jill Roundhouse's mouth.

Chapter Nineteen
The Good Part

Irwin leaned back. Another chunky load lay on the floor between his ankles. Watching Tabby take Daddy's vomit and recycle it had almost been too much for Irwin's pecker. He felt like taking a nap now that he had spent such a heavy amount of wet change.

Irwin wiped his brow and sat up straight. His jowls trembled with delight. He typed out a message for the chat. Even though all of Daddy's attention was focused on Tabby, Irwin wanted to send him a bit of encouragement. Before he sent some money over, that was.

ARM&RMBLE69: Whoa! That was amazing! This has been such an incredible show!

BASKERVILLESTORMENT: This isn't even the good part! The final task is next! I don't even know what she's going to do!

COINSLOT: don't think she'll do it.

GUTALT2003: Dumbass. She'll do it. She's gotten this far.

COINSLOT: I don't know. I think she'll back

out.

ARM&RUMBLE69: She'll do it. I know she will. She's fucking amazing.

YUYUY777: You have a crush?

ARM&RUMBLE69: Sure. She's hot.

ODDBALLODD32ILL: Eww. She's covered in shit.

ARM&RUMBLE69: Are you telling me you don't jack it while you watch this?

ODDBALLODD32ILL: No way. I just watch it for the lolz.

YUYUY777: Pussy.

GUTALT2003: Pussy.

ARM&RUMBLE69: Pussy.

COINSLOT: Dude, uv got 2 start beating off 2 this shit. That's the whole point.

ODDBALLODD32ILL: I thought the point was to see how far people would go for folks they love.

COINSLOT: ur acting like this is a social experiment.

YUYUY777: Or a fucking flash mob. Remember those?

BASKERVILLESTORMENT: Yeah, we all jerk off to this shit. I mean, it's way better than porno. I love watching bitches cry. I love it. Makes me feel like I'm getting back at all the cunts that ever got in my way.

YUYUY777: Women are queens. Just kidding.

COINSLOT: I'd love to fuck her. I'd love to

make her swallow my fucking puke.

YUYUY777: Did you see she pissed herself? I wish we got a close up on that.

COINSLOT: I see enough of that on Xvideos. I'm more into the tears.

BASKERVILLESTORMENT: Has anyone here ever raped someone?

GUTALT2003: No. I'd never do anything we watch on this stream in real life. I just like to watch. I don't wanna cross that line, you know?

ODDBALLODD32ILL: See? That's what I'm saying.

GUTALT2003: Pussy. You couldn't rape a slut even if you tried.

ODDBALLODD32ILL: Jesus. What'd I do to you, dude?

GUTALT2003: I'm just messing with you. It's a joke, not a dick.

ODDBALLODD32ILL: Fuck. Sorry. Hard to read sarcasm.

ARM&RUMBLE69: She's still taking in all that vomit. She's so hot.

COINSLOT: I raped someone.

YUYUY777: She's super-hot. In a MILF-y way.

GUTALT2003: She's too old for me. I like them younger.

YUYUY777: How young.

GUTALT2003: Can't say. How cool are you?

YUYUY777: I'm going to send you some videos I've got. Hold up.

ODDBALLODD32ILL: I still don't feel like jerking off to this. But it is entertaining.

ARM&RUMBLE69: Just try it.

COINSLOT: Hey, YUY. Send me some ofof those videos 2.

ARM&RUMBLE69: If you try it you may like it. It took me awhile to really get into it but now I can't cum unless someone is crying. It's fucking great. Daddy is too good to us.

Chapter Twenty
Sober Up, Buttercup

Tabby lifted her head and wiped her mouth with the back of her hand. Her mouth was filled with pennies, but she was content. She had completed the third task.

"I underestimated you, Tabs." Daddy cheered. "Bravo! Bravo!"

"Let's finish... this." Tabby declared.

"Oh, Tabby. I'd love that. But first, just let me congratulate you. You did such a grand job! Really!"

"I don't care. Stop. Please." Tabby's voice was cold and medical. She had lost the ability to emote halfway through her vomit-soup ordeal. "I just want to see my daughter."

"And you will." Daddy promised. "But don't you think you deserve a little treat before you do?"

"No. I don't want that. Please, stop stalling. Fourth task. Let's do it."

"I must insist that you give yourself a moment." Daddy said smarmily. "After all, you've worked so hard. Everyone that

152

accomplishes a great task deserves a great reward."

Daddy held up his hand and beckoned for Markos. The brute wandered over and scooped Tabby up beneath her arms. With a grunt, he hefted her to her wavering feet. He held her steady in front of Daddy.

"You deserve... one good punch."

Tabby screwed her eyebrows together.

"You can hit me... anywhere you like. As hard as you like. Look," Daddy raised his mask up and exposed his soft face, "you can even get me right in the kisser."

Tabby waited for the catch.

"You must hate me." Daddy said. "I know. What I've done to you is... well... it's unforgivable. But you won't get your revenge. You won't get to kill me. This isn't like the movies. You'll finish the final task... I'll give you Riley... and you'll never see me again. Ever. The police won't find me. You've got no chance of stopping this from happening to someone else. So, enjoy your moment of retaliation. Hit me, Tabs. And make it count!"

Daddy leaned in and puckered up his lips, as if he expected a smooch.

Tabby reeled her arm back and struck with all her might. The punch was weak. It thudded limply against Daddy's face. It sounded like a dry fart.

Tabby felt more ashamed than ever before.

She had envisioned hurting Daddy and his comrade so many times in the last few hours... and now that she had an opportunity she had wasted it. But her body just wasn't in the mood to fight. It was sore and drained and frail.

All she could muster was the slightest of thumps against his jawline.

Daddy lowered his mask, concealing his rabid smile. He chuckled and put his fists against his hips. "Good effort, baby. Good try."

Tabby moaned. Her body was parched and there were no tears left in her. But she wished, more than ever, that she could weep.

"You ready for the last task?" Daddy asked.

Tabby nodded.

"Come with me." He turned and stamped toward the door. He even held it open for her. Ever the perfect gentleman.

Tabby and Markos left the house. Markos was close behind her, digging his yellowed nails into her shoulder. He led her toward the gravel drive, where their van was parked.

She could see her child.

Seeing the little girl made Tabby's heart stutter.

She was tied to a lawn-chair with duct tape and her head was concealed behind a potato sack. She was set out on the ground in front of the headlights of the van. As if she was a spectator at a parade. Her little fingers worked at the knots around her wrists, but they didn't seem to budge.

Tabby lurched toward her daughter, but Markos pulled her back with a grunt. "Stay!" He commanded and threw her to the ground. Naked, her skin was vulnerable to the pebbles and gravel chunks around her. She felt her knees scrape open and her palms fill with bits of stone. One of her nail-less fingers broke open against a jagged rock. It squirted a thin jet stream of fresh blood. She hugged the ground and drew her knees to her breasts.

Daddy walked around her, moving backwards so he could capture her for the audience.

"You're almost to the finish line, sweetie!" He declared. He reached behind his back and pulled a handgun out from beneath his duster. He carried it in his left hand while the Uzi dangled from his right.

"Markos. Step aside."

Markos did as he was commanded. He ambled away from Tabby, leaving her unattended.

She scrabbled up to her feet. Blood dripped down her legs and from her clenched fists.

Daddy took the lawn chair and dragged it around so that the girl was facing her mother. The girl couldn't see regardless of the sack-mask, but still it felt cruel. Tabby knew she didn't look at all like the mother Riley remembered. She was naked, coated in fluids, and wild-eyed. She looked like a zombie from a cheap horror movie.

"What do I have to do?" Tabby asked. "What's the last task?"

"It's the same for every player." Daddy intoned. "You have to prove that the life in front of you is a life worth saving."

Daddy tossed the handgun. It landed in front of Tabby's feet.

He jerked the Uzi up and prodded the side of the child's head with its barrel. Beneath her mask, the child began to screech. She jerked against her restraints, rocking her chair back and forth.

"It's not enough to take a strangers life in exchange for hers." Daddy said. "You have to take your own too."

Tabby felt as if the world had stopped moving.

"W-what?"

"If you kill yourself, Tabby... we let Riley go. We untie her and we leave. Randy's probably on his way by now after that phone call. She'll be safe and he'll watch over her. But that only happens if you do what needs to be done. If you swallow a bullet, she lives. If you don't, I blow her head to pieces. I'm not going to chop off a limb. I don't give a shit about what happens to her left leg. I don't care about any of her arms or legs. What I care about is this: how far are you willing to go for her? How far is too far? Have you drawn a line yet?"

Tabby shook her head. "This... this isn't what we agreed on."

"We agreed you'd play my game. This is how it's played. The final task is always the same. Either you kill yourself... or I kill her."

"Stop it." Tabby stated. "Just stop it. Why? Why are you even doing this? What did I ever do to you? What did she ever do? She's a child! She is a CHILD!"

Daddy shook his head. "You gotta make a choice, Tabby. You or her. If you choose her, we'll leave. We'll take her with us too. You'll have a lot of explaining to do... but you'll be alive to tell the tale. Which do you prefer? Total annihilation or a living daughter?"

"You're sick. You both are sick." Tabby seethed.

"I know." Daddy poked the child once more. "I'm going to give you to the count of five."

"No."

"One."

"No. Please."

"Two."

Tabby stooped over and picked up the gun. She held it up and pointed it toward Daddy.

"Three." Daddy drove the muzzle of the Uzi into the side of the wailing girl's head. As he did so, Markos pulled out a handgun and directed it toward the child's head.

Even if Tabby shot one of them, the other would kill her daughter.

"Four." Daddy said.

Tabby's fingers shook. Her breath came out in raspy strands.

"Fi—"

Tabby tipped her head back and put the gun beneath her chin.

She pulled the trigger.

Chapter Twenty-One
Cold and Dead

Daddy watched as her face exploded. Shredded meat and teeth flew into the air ahead of her, along with a cloud of red mist. Tabby tittered on her feet before falling face down in the gravel. She clutched the gun close to her chest, as if it was a locket she held dearly.

Daddy paused, watching her still body. He dropped the Uzi from the girl's head and stepped toward Tabby.

She had done it.

Just as he expected... she had proved to him that she loved her daughter.

"Shit, man!" Markos clapped his hands together and stepped in front of the camera. "That does it! Thank you guys for making this our highest viewed show yet!"

Daddy didn't listen to Markos's platitudes. Instead, he looked up towards the grey-blue sky and smiled beneath his mask. A job well done was reward enough for him. He couldn't believe how well things had gone. It was as if God was on his side.

Daddy was glad that all of their footage was

permanent. He would re-watch this day over and over again. Just like his junkie followers, he was truly addicted to the violence and the pain he caused.

He returned to earth and looked toward Markos.

"And special shout-out to ARM&RUMBLE69 for suggesting we do something with puke." Markos said and gave the camera a goofy 'OK' symbol with his fingers. "That was fucking nasty and you're a total sicko. We love all of you... and we can't wait to see you again next time!"

He reached over and turned the camera off for Daddy. He unhooked the phone from his strap and began to thumb through it.

"How much did we make?" Daddy asked.

"A lot." Markos grunted.

"Record setting?"

"Yeah. This one was big. The usual suspects were in the chat but... a lot of people watched the stream. And they paid up." Markos clicked his tongue. "You know, Peter... I fuckin' love what we do—"

A gunshot ripped through the air.

The bullet tore into Markos's throat and sprayed blood across Daddy's mask. Daddy backpedaled, dropped his Uzi, and released a yowl.

Markos clawed at his opened throat. His mask was still on, concealing his fear and panic. But

Daddy could see his eyes. Markos was more afraid than he had ever been in his entire, miserable life.

Markos fell to his knees and scrabbled for breath. The bottom of his mask was oozing blood. Hot, red, fluid jetted out of his wound in rapid bursts. It sprayed between his fingers and decorated the gravel.

"Uhhhhhhh!" Markos groaned. "Uhhhhhhh! Haaa-alp!"

Another gunshot pounded through the stagnant air. This bullet slammed into the back of Markos's head. It poked a dime-sized hole through his cranium and burst out of the front of his mask, cracking it like an egg. Brain-gravy spilled out of the fissure in a fuming shower.

Markos collapsed. His wheezing screams were halted, and his body lay still.

Daddy stared at him in abject horror.

Markos was his best friend. His partner. His buddy.

No one else knew Daddy's depravity, or his business. No one else understood what Daddy felt or just how sinister his compulsions were.

Markos was his mirror image, even if he was as dumb as a box of rocks and just as sturdy. Without him, Daddy felt entirely alone.

He looked up toward Markos's killer.

He was surprised to see that Tabby had crawled back up to her feet.

Her face was destroyed. The bullet had torn through the space between her nose and her lower jaw. A cave-like hole exposed the inner workings of her head. Strands of muscle, red flesh, and pumping blood sluiced from the injury. Above the wound, her eyes had turned crimson. They were crazed with anger and pain.

She didn't kill herself. Oh, God. She's still alive!

Daddy leapt backwards. Away from his dead comrade and away from the captive child. All Daddy wanted to do was get away from the ghoulish woman that had him in her sights.

Another gunshot rang out, like the bell over a gothic cathedral.

It hit the interior of Daddy's van, cracking his computer screen and sending sparks flying.

Daddy crawled in and scuttled toward the front seat. As he went, a fourth bullet trimmed his calf. Blood shot out of the wound and painted the backside of the passenger seat.

Daddy yelped and crawled into the driver's seat, dragging his injured leg with him. He cranked the car to life and whirled it around. He felt the bumper connect with the police-cruiser.

Daddy hit the gas and barreled toward the ghastly woman. She stepped forward, not fearing the van and its power. Confidently, she squeezed the trigger.

Nothing happened.

The gun was empty.

A smile broke out beneath Daddy's mask.

The van bore down on Tabby with the brute strength of an animal. She spun through the air and slammed into the ground. Her left arm snapped beneath her, pushing out a white bone-shaft which sprayed blood and black gunk across the gravel.

The van rolled over her. Its tires upended the flesh of her chest and crushed her ribs. Daddy laughed uproariously as the van jumped up and down on top of Tabby's body.

"Teach *you* to fuck with me!" Daddy shouted through the pain flaring up his leg. "I'm a God, you cunt! I'm a fucking GOD!"

The van roared down the drive and into the road.

Daddy drove away from Tabby's farm, laughing as he went.

Chapter Twenty-Two
An Awful Homecoming

When Randy pulled up to his farm, he was surprised by the carnage. A man he did not know was lying on the ground, his head as open as a book. A ways away from him, a child was strapped to a lawn chair. She was rocking hysterically back and forth, screaming so loud Randy could hear her even though his windows were rolled up. But what really shocked him was his wife. Tabby was laid out on the ground, her chest concave and her arm broken. Her face looked like a slab of chewed-up meat. A gun lay a few yards away from her busted fingers.

Randy threw the car into park and jumped out. Ignoring the pleading child, he knelt down by his wife and cradled her as best he could. He could hear her bones grinding together in her broken chest. He realized, when he saw her opened face, that he wished she were dead. Because death was a mercy compared to the agony she was enduring.

"Oh, God... Tabby!" Randy declared. "What happened? Jesus."

Tabby spoke. Her words were so slurred, they

were almost illegible. Her tongue was a smoking hunk of tangled roots. Her teeth had all been reduced to shards. The words were coming from her throat, and even that was distorted. Her lungs were filling with liquid death even as she spoke. Every movement caused another spear of bone to rupture yet another organ.

"I..." Tabby managed with great effort. "I... did... it... for... her."

"What did you do? Tabby, who did this? Tell me!"

"I did... it... for... Riiiii-lee."

Blood began to ease its way out of her nostrils. Her red eyes turned pale, and her body went tranquil in his hands. She was dead.

Randy found himself treated to an internal montage. He remembered courting and wooing Tabby. He remembered taking her on spontaneous dates to trashy flea-markets. He remembered carrying her into their house after their honey-moon, and he remembered making love to her for the first time. He remembered the way she sang in the shower, and the way she laughed when she got mad, as if her anger was driving her crazy. He began to remember every little mole on her body, and every time she complained about the grey hairs she found on her head.

He remembered when she was pregnant with—

—Riley.

He looked away from his wife's remains and toward the captive child. Of course, whatever had happened had been about Riley. Who else?

He suddenly realized that his wife was a hero. She had givin her own life in exchange for Riley. And she had done so all while Randy was hiding at his parents' house.

He felt his teeth dig into his lower lip. He needed to repress his shame. It wasn't important. What was important was his daughter.

Randy bolted across the driveway and began to help the child out of her restraints. He worked the bungee-cords lose and used his compact knife to cut away the duct tape. After hanging the folded blade back on his belt-loop, he ceremoniously removed the potato sack.

The blinded child turned her head toward him, as if she could see out of her scabrous eyes.

"Riley! It's me! It's your pa—"

Randy looked down at the child. His heart stopped in his chest.

Tabby would be forgiven for assuming that the child in the photo was her daughter. But the Polaroid Daddy had given her hid some truths from view. It was a shaky shot taken in the back of a shadowy van, after all.

Randy had the advantage of sunlight.

He could spot the differences right away.

This child didn't have a birthmark on her neck.

This child had an upturned nose.

This child didn't have freckles.

This child had blonde roots.

And this child was two years older than Riley.

Abruptly, Randy seized the blind child by the shoulders and shook her.

"Who are you? What's your name?"

"I'm Riley." The girl responded in a voice that sounded nothing like his daughter.

"No! You tell me who you are *this instant*!" Randy scolded, sounding more like a schoolteacher than a grieving parent.

"I'm Riley!" The girl declared. "Please! Don't hurt me! Please."

Randy shook her violently. His fingers dug into her arms. "You tell me who you are! You tell me right now!"

"I'm Riley! I'm Riley!" The child proclaimed. "Please! They told me to say my name was Riley! They told me that's my new name! Please! That's who I am! I'm Riley! I'm Riley!"

Randy released her and stepped back.

His jaw hung open and his eyes welled up with tears.

"I'm Riley! I'm Riley!" The child sobbed. "I'm Riley! That's my name now! I'm not Sarah... I'm *RILEY*!"

Chapter Twenty-Three
Mother's Comfort

Daddy arrived at his home in a stupor. He had
dressed his wound all on his own, having
pilfered supplies from a pharmacy and setting
up a make-shift medical center in the back of his
van. The van smelled like piss and blood, but he
had done a pretty good job given the
circumstances. Still, he walked with a limp and
his head was foggy with pain. He made a mental
note to check his dad's cabinet for pain meds. He
always had something that would do the trick.
Even a dandruff flake of cocaine would be
appreciated.

Daddy wandered into his room and flicked the
light on.

He was surprised to see his mother waiting for
him.

She was sitting on his bed in the darkness.

"Whoa. Mom." He straightened his back and
tried to conceal his limp. He had changed
outfits. He was now wearing a fresh pair of jeans
and a superhero tee. His hair was greased back
with sweat and his eyes were baggy. He looked
hungover.

He could explain a hangover. He couldn't explain a bullet through his calf.

He was going to need to look up an unlicensed doctor online. He needed to find someone to take care of his wound without leaving a record.

"Hello, Peter." His mother said and smiled.

Peter stumbled into the room and took a seat at his writing desk. He put his hands behind his head and tried to look relaxed. "What's up, Mom? Are you doing okay?"

"Where have you been these last two days?" His mom asked. She was a small and round woman with brown hair and a tubby frame.

"Oh. Markos and I went on a little impromptu road trip. He's... he's visiting some friends a few states over and I offered to drive him."

He'd figure out a way to explain his friend's disappearance later. His head was throbbing.

"If you don't mind, Ma, I'd actually like to get some rest before doing my homework."

"Baby." His mother pursed her wrinkled lips. "I went on your computer."

Peter felt the air in the room drop. His blood froze over in his veins.

"What?" He asked. "Th-that's private."

"Well, hun... your dad was on our computer, and I really needed to look up something for work and... I figured you wouldn't mind." She shook her head. "I opened it up and saw... I saw..." She shuddered. "Some of them were *children."*

Peter's heart thumped like a rabbit in a trap. His gums went dry, and his legs began to jitter. He felt both embarrassed and frightened. He began to berate himself. Obviously, in his hurry, he had left a tab open. A file filled with atrocities. Despite all his passwords and his security... he had been dumb enough to leave his computer open and his notebook filled with his information and pass-keys out beside it.

"I mean, children? Peter? Toddlers? And they... the things they were being forced to..." She shook her head. It was too much for her to bear, he could see. His mother had found his dirty secret, and now she was airing it out.

What was she going to do? Call the cops? Tell his dad?

Or was there a chance she would keep it between them. Maybe he could convince her he wanted to change. That he'd get better. She didn't seem to know about any of the Daddy Torture-Fuck shit. Just the porn. And that was bad enough. But maybe there was a chance he could get away from all of this.

Peter turned up the waterworks. He began to cry and sniffle, as if he had simply been caught with his hand in a cookie jar.

"I don't know, Ma. It's like... it's like someone else takes over. And I can't stop him."

"*Children*, Peter." His mother shook her head.

"I'm... I'm so sorry. I don't know why I do it. I guess I have problems. I guess I'm... I'm unwell." He pleaded. "I feel terrible when I do it. But I can't stop. I need... I need *help*, Mama."

She sighed. "I wish I knew how to help you, son."

"Please." He got down on his knees, hands clasped together. "We can figure it out, can't we? Can't we, Mama? We can burn my computer and... and I'll never go back on it. I'll pray too. I'll even go back to church. Maybe God can make me better. Maybe he can heal me!"

His mother began to nod. A smile broke out across her craggy face. She reached out and touched his warm cheek with her right hand. "Oh, son. I don't think God cares about you anymore."

Peter's face fell.

Then, he saw that his mother had also found the handgun he kept under his bed.

She held it up and fired directly into the space between his eyes.

The back of Peter's head exploded. Blood and brain matter flew out behind him and coated the wall.

His body fell and shook against the floor, as if he was having a seizure.

And then all was quiet.

Finally... all was quiet.

For the Sake Of

THE END

Afterword

I'll keep this brief. *For the Sake Of* was the fourth novel I published, but the second one I released on my own. I was still learning the ropes, in a lot of ways. So even though it was well-liked, I always wanted to put a fresh coat of paint on it. I actually believed it needed more to it.

Well, going back and re-reading it, I disagree with that sentiment. I think this book is still one of the darkest things I've written. It didn't need a re-write... it just needed an upgrade. If the first edition was a DVD, I'd like to think that this version is a fancy new Blu-ray, released by a fun label.

Not something like *Criterion*... but... *maybe Unearthed Films.*

I digress. Anyways, if you want to spot the differences between the first version and this, then it might be a futile exercise. Yes, I fixed some grammar, edited some overlong sentences, and used my lucky thesaurus on some repeated words. Otherwise... this is exactly the same experience that initial readers had when they picked up the book in the early days of 2022.

Wow. Doesn't feel like that was all too long ago, huh? Since then, I've published over twenty books. Whew. I should definitely take a break someday.

But not yet.

I just published an Italian splatter throwback called *Hell,* I'm writing a revenge thriller, and I'm planning out the next "Ten Day Challenge" with a few authors I respect and love.

It's strange to think that when I first published *For the Sake Of...* I wasn't close friends with authors like Lucas Mangum, Christy Aldridge, or Brian Berry. I didn't have my circle yet, and I was sort of bumbling around in the scene looking for a seat that wasn't taken.

Anyways, this book was inspired by flicks like *Phonebooth* and *Would You Rather?* I like indie films about people being put in uncomfortable or dangerous situations, all for the benefit of a strange benefactor. Some folks have said this book reminded them of *Saw,* and I definitely see that. But I don't really think I'll ever do "trap" type kills in this series. I like the idea of the horror and torture being more "situational".

Another thing people have said is that they didn't love how two-dimensional the villains are but, that's the point. The bad guys are supposed to just be anonymous, online trolls. Keyboard warriors who revel in abuse and humiliation. That said, I heard those concerns... and that's why *For the Sake Of (2)* focuses almost exclusively on the baddies.

And if you thought this book was nasty, just wait until I re-release (2) in May! That book even makes me a little seasick. Writing it was a painful experience.

Like pulling out your own fingers.

I'm dreading re-reading it just to prepare it for its new release.

A quick thank you to all the folks who read and recommended this book! Mique Watson, Meghin, KillerBunny, and many more. There were a lot of folks that discussed this book on Instagram and YouTube right when it came out. I can only hope it'll find a similarly loving audience once again.

Thank you to Aron Beauregard and Daniel Volpe, for letting me steal your names for the bar scene.

Thank you, as always, to Lucas Mangum. I wouldn't feel so at home if it wasn't for your hyping, your advice, and your understanding.

From Utah, with love...
Judith Sonnet
3/28/2023

Printed in Great Britain
by Amazon